THE DAY MARLENE DIETRICH DIED

THE
DAY
MARLENE
DIETRICH
DIED

STORIES
BY
RACHEL
WYATT

OOLICHAN BOOKS
LANTZVILLE, BRITISH COLUMBIA
CANADA
1996

Canadian Cataloguing in Publication Data

Wyatt, Rachel, 1929-
    The day Marlene Dietrich died

    ISBN 0-88982-161-5

    1. Dietrich, Marlene--Fiction. I. Title.
PS8595.Y3D39 1996   C813'.54   C96-910589-4
PR9199.3 W88D39 1996

The cover art is by kind permission of AKG Photo, London for
the black & white photograph of Marlene Dietrich and Ron
Smith for the use of the painting of Marlene Dietrich by John
Lim.

Oolichan Books acknowledges the support received for its pub-
lishing program from the Canada Council's Block Grants program, the British Columbia Ministry of Small Business, Tour-
ism and Culture, and the Department of Canadian Heritage.

Published by
Oolichan Books
P.O. Box 10
Lantzville, British Columbia
Canada V0R 2H0

Printed in Canada by
Morriss Printing Company Limited
Victoria, British Columbia

To the women in my life

Acknowledgements

The idea for this collection was conceived at the Banff Centre for the Arts on the day Marlene Dietrich died in May, 1992. My thanks are due to the Banff Centre for its benign influence on my work and for giving me the chance to meet so many fine writers. I am most grateful to Edna Alford for her careful editing of these stories and for her kind encouragement.

Several of the stories have appeared in other publications: "The Hobby" and "Her Voice" (as "Come Back to Me, Peter") were published in *Quarry;* "A Wall of Bright Stone" in *Grain*; "Bride of the Sea" and "A Fairly Fatal Woman" (as "Tea at the Ritz") in *Room of One's Own.*

Contents

HER
VOICE

"Well," she said.

"It was a long time ago," he said.

"You never did get over it."

"You never got over it."

She pulled the newspaper round to her side of the table and looked at the photograph. The face was well-lit, the bone structure too good to be true, the hair so blonde, the glance remote.

"This is an old picture," she said.

He said nothing.

"She wore a kind of body stocking made of wire like a cage. That's how she looked slim."

He picked up his cup and put his face down to it, hiding from truth as he had done all his life.

"She slept with more men than most people've had hot dinners. Anyone in trousers. Even women."

He smashed his cup down and broke the saucer into three pieces.

"She was a bent old skeleton in a wheelchair."

The house around them appeared to close in. The

wallpaper chosen by her, pink flowers on a trellis, became a cage. The drapes, washed just last week because grease and flies and splashes from the sink
attached themselves to cotton so easily, looked dirty
again. The plates, Summer, Fall, Winter, on the shelf
over the sideboard lost their gloss.

She had loved him in all the seasons once.

The clock he had brought back for her from Swit-
zerland hung there two feet from the plates, telling time
as if they needed to be told how quickly it was passing.
The cuckoo, as arthritic as Peter himself, only came
out of its little house on the hours and then slowly. One
of these times, it would remain inside and let them
know that it was mortal too.

"I've always hated that clock," she said to remind
him of the time he had run away.

It was twenty years or so after the war, after he had
first seen HER in Paris in 1945. Twenty years! Back to
Europe. One day he'd taken the holiday money from
their account and gone off on his own to Germany. To
that first concert SHE had given in her homeland. He
hadn't been able to get a seat in the hall in Munich but
he'd heard the shouts of the audience. Through the
whole concert he stood in the crowded foyer. Sixty-two
curtain calls. Sixty-two! A modest person would have
taken three or four bows and then left the stage. He
should have seen then that she was vain and vainglori-
ous and could never have looked at him.

But he had used their holiday money to go there
alone, to see HER, to be recognised. The futile dream
of a man in his forties. And then he'd gone on to Swit-
zerland because, he said later, it was there.

"What made you think I'd want a thing like that?"

she'd asked when he got back and handed her the clock wrapped in brown paper.

Now he stayed silent, only turned the page so he could look at her picture again. And then he folded it over to read *Ukraine Hands Over Nuclear Arsenal, Left-handers Have More Accidents, Boy Killed By Cougar, Moratorium Declared On Cod-fishing.*

"This can't change things," she said and leaned across to pick up the pieces of the saucer.

There were none of those scrappy fragments this time, only whole sections. Some things broke whole and others split into a million fragments hard to get up, hard to get out of corners or out of cloth or the rug. At times she'd been afraid to go about the house in bare feet.

"So she's dead," Myra repeated.

And again he was silent.

Still glamorous at seventy, at eighty, she was fine in her way, Myra thought, revered, quoted, loved. Marlene had swung those legs, sung those songs, and maybe in the privacy of her quiet room, in her old age, she had hummed along to her old records and recalled the acclaim of millions.

"Some of us got veins from standing around washing other people's dishes," Myra said as she stood up, the saucer in her hand.

"Come back," he said to her. "Come back here."

"Do you think," she shouted back over her shoulder, "that she would have moved here, to this place, lived in a house like this, made jellied salad for the Curling Club supper, sung at Rotary concerts, asked them to call her Marl for short!"

In all honesty, she knew that was not his dream. To bring Marlene Dietrich to Winouski. He could never have thought that. All he had imagined and had gone on imagining, was the brilliant fireworks of a few flaming weeks of passion. *Have you any cigarettes, Payter? I'll get my own. Payter! Payter! Komm zu mir zurück!*

And the poor dumb cluck thought she had sung that song for him.

Myra kept on walking towards the back door carrying the broken saucer. It was most likely his turn to be right but she was not, on this day, about to give him that satisfaction.

She opened the back door and there was Thea advancing through the gap in the hedge. Thea was long-faced as if a relative had died or a dog had been run over. She was followed by her old man, Jim, known all over the neighbourhood for borrowing things and not returning them.

"You've heard?"

Neighbours got too familiar if you let them. Here they were, not even waiting to be asked, marching right over, just because an old actress had died. As if they were family, as if they had rights. Jim was grinning to let Myra know it hadn't been his idea. Thea had most likely said, "Let's go and comfort poor Pete." And so they had come over. An errand of mercy!

Jim went up to Pete and patted his shoulder. Sympathy. Even a kind of love. Something secret between men. Myra saw it and hated it. Hated them for the moment.

Thea nodded towards Jim and Peter as if to say, Men! Her hair was stiffened into curls and she was wearing a white blouse with a silver brooch at the neck and had put on her navy skirt with the silver belt, not her usual morning wear at all. She was making an occasion out of someone else's trouble. That was Thea all over. If she had not been so good-hearted besides, Myra would have closed the door to her long ago.

Thea looked at the broken saucer still in Myra's hand.

"I've decided to glue it," Myra said.

"She was old," Thea stated. "It can't have been a good life, these last years."

Oh and is yours, Myra wanted to ask. Is yours? Here we all are, steps away from the old folks home, from dying alone, unvisited, from going slowly ga-ga, without speech or sense. This is a good life!

"It's a nice day," she said.

She knew they had come to hear the story again. Or maybe not to hear it but to touch Pete because he had once, almost, touched HER.

Anyone would think he'd won that medal for seeing her, watching her sing. And not for crossing a minefield on his own. Soldiers! They fought and owned the world for a time. Where was the bravery! What had he done? She was the enemy, Marlene, hers as well as his. And he had lusted after this German woman and seen her close enough to touch and she had smiled at him across a crowd of autograph hunters and said, "Where are you from, soldier?"

He had replied, "Canada." And that had been enough to drive him half crazy for the rest of his life.

And then SHE had said, "Canada is so cold, isn't it?"

Before he could reply, a pudgy-faced actor had come along and stood nearby leaning on the wall watching her talk to him, and there was a sense of menace in the way that Frenchman leaned against the wall. Another Frenchman, Maurice-every-little-breeze-seems-to-whisper-Louise-Chevalier, had come out of the stage door and joined him. Pete, overwhelmed, had backed away as if from royalty, not able to realise that those two were only men like himself.

Doctors had said back in those first years after the return, after peace, that Pete was suffering from the shock of that step-by-step journey across the mined field. *Death might have taken him in any moment of that twenty-minute walk, Mrs. Chebs.*

But even then, even before he recovered enough to go back to work and to make love and to be there with her, she knew what had made him ill. It was knowing what he had lost, as if one of his legs or an arm had been blown off. That feeling followed him through his days like a ghost: If he had put himself forward, spoken out, he might have taken that woman's hand and led her away to a room somewhere where there was wine, where there were cigarettes. There would have been no need for music.

Jean, the actor, Jean Gabin, the man leaning against the wall, was Marlene's lover. Peter learned that later, but he knew, Myra knew he had known, that in that moment, if he had gone forward, SHE could have been his. He could have led her away from those Frenchmen and he had not. And he suffered more from that retreat than if he had run away from the enemy, more than if he had turned at the edge of the minefield and said to his sergeant, "I'm not going across there," and got shot after all as a coward. And on some days she knew he wished he had.

In his mind still, old and slow as he was, he was not a retired Post Office driver, not a well-respected member of the Union, ex-president of the Kiwanis and father of two, he was the man who could have made love to Marlene Dietrich.

Jim was saying, "Remember that scene where James Stewart had hold of her leg? And then they had that great fight."

Thea preferred to recall Gabin. "I saw him once in some old French movie and he scarcely ever took his cap off. A flat tweed cap. In the house. In a cafe. Talking to his girl. And he lit one cigarette from another. I don't remember movies I've seen. But I do remember that."

Peter smiled softly, listening, stroking his own memories as they talked.

In a minute, because she couldn't help herself, Myra would offer them coffee, get out the cookies. But first they had to harp on his dream, Pete's old dream.

You dreamer, she had said to him long ago in the days when she thought he might get over it. *You know it wasn't real. She would never have gone with you.*

But he never had known that. Forever in his mind the conversation begun that night continued, repeated itself like a stuck record. On and on, lines being added and changed in his head.

Cold in Canada, isn't it?
We manage to keep warm.
How do you do that, soldier?
Peter, my name is Peter.
How do you keep warm in Canada, eh Peter?
First of all we have a drink.
Have you got any whisky, Peter?
Sure do.
My place or yours?

Peter said now, "It was her voice. Not the words. The words didn't matter, but her voice."

Jim had once said to Myra, joking after a few drinks, "Does he call you Marlene when he makes love?"

She had smiled and her heart had been chipped on that day. Not broken but chipped like a cup that wouldn't be much use any more. Chipped again like the day her old friend Amber had gone off without saying where.

Thea said to comfort him, "Let's see your medal, Pete."

Myra got up and said, "Coffee. Two with and two without, right," and went to the kitchen.

Fortunately Pete was modest and they wouldn't press him. In a fit of anger, years ago, after he had thrown the Spring plate against the wall and shattered it, she had put his medal in the oven and turned the heat up. It hadn't melted but had come out charred-looking and the ribbon was ruined. When it was cool she'd returned it to its case. And he had never said anything.

After Thea and Jim left, after Peter had gone outside to chop wood and cut the bit of grass at the front, Myra went upstairs to make the beds. She opened her closet and looked at the clothes inside. She had never owned any pencil-slim suits or hats that perched on the side of her head or spangly gowns that fitted where they touched. She had never worn silver shoes or owned a diamond bracelet. She had never, that she could remember, been thin.

Later that evening, when she got back from Bingo, he was sitting at the table, looking at the newspaper, still wearing his black tie. She wanted to shout at him, to tell him he had wasted tons of emotion, his and hers, on that woman. She wanted to scream out in anguish but had no idea how to go about it. She opened her mouth and nothing came out but a squeak.

Besides, she had just won thirty dollars and she knew in her heart there was no use in being jealous of the dead. Perhaps it was time to forgive him for all those times in bed when he had imagined her stocky legs to be long and slim, her hair loose and blonde, and had kissed her so as not to hear a different voice.

She put her hand on his arm and said, "It's all right." But she couldn't stop his tears. She went upstairs to let him mourn in peace. While she was undressing, she tried to sing, *Peter, Peter, komm zu mir zurück*, but it didn't sound right. She never had been able to carry a tune.

A
WALL
OF
BRIGHT
STONE

Sharon looked down at the grave and wished she had come on vacation alone. She could have said, *Not this year, Kim. I'm meeting someone over there.* She could have said cruelly, *I don't want to go to Europe with you again.* But here she was, one more time, watching, waiting, wanting to be on the move.

Jess at the office had said, "You two always go on vacation together." And Sharon had almost snapped back, *Wanna make something of it!* but instead had only smiled as if she was doing Kim a favour and said, "The single supplement on these packages is prohibitive."

She shuffled her feet around on the ground feeling for the imprints of the important people who had stood here in mourning only a few days before. Old film stars, politicians, the mayor of the city. The grass was rough and the trees still, but a chill wind was blowing round the little cemetery. Perhaps it always did.

"It's not as if you'd known her," Sharon said to Kim.

They were wasting time at $10.50 an hour. She'd

calculated the price of the package, airfare and accommodation, not counting meals and spending money, and divided it by the number of waking hours in their vacation. $10.50 an hour each! There was so much to see and do in Berlin, and she liked to follow the guidebook and take in as many points of interest as she could. She wouldn't be in Germany ever again most likely. And here she was, having spent all that money, catching her death of cold in a graveyard.

"My father knew her once," Kim said.

"Whose didn't?" Sharon replied.

Kim didn't hear, she was bending over, her thighs tight in the pink skirt, reading the names on the floral offerings.

"They called her the best-dressed man in Hollywood," she said, looking up, smiling the crooked smile that made her face into a series of triangles, elongated ones for eyes, wide one for a mouth. Her hair was cut so that it hung in fronds round her face. Her lips were rounded and smooth with silky gloss, carnation. There were carnations on the grave too.

We've had a lot of good times, Sharon would say to Kim this coming November or December. *You'll find someone else to go on vacation with*. And then she, travelling alone, would have a chance to get to know the people, to throw out her few phrases, be invited into homes, be less of a stranger. And finally she would find him, the man in the garden.

She had always known he was there, in a foreign place, her perfect companion. Somewhere he sat among his flowers near a wall made of bright stone, an apricot or nectarine tree espaliered against it. He was reading poems in a thin book, murmuring lines to him-

self. Seeing her he would look up and say, *O time stand
still, stay happy hours,* the phrase a password by
which she would know him. It was only a question of
going to him on her own and saying, *Here I am,* and
life would be a new and bright affair, no longer repeti-
tive, no longer a wintry stretch of time in which her
competence at work was her main satisfaction.

Sharon hadn't bothered to ask Kim's opinion about
this year's change in plan. Kim would have chosen
Helsinki and Leningrad for the strangeness of it, paying no attention to the fact that neither of them knew
anything about Finland, that Russia was in turmoil,
that no meals were included and that the hotels were
said to be short on the usual conveniences like soap
and toilet paper.

She simply told Kim that they would take *Three
German Cities for the Price of Two* because the climate
was similar and they could take the clothes they had
planned to wear in Yugoslavia. She had packed her
uncrushable blue suit, three blouses that matched, her
necklace of lapis chips, and two pantsuits. Her gold
chains. She was wearing the grey pantsuit now with
her red blouse and a gold S on the lapel. Comfortable
sight-seeing shoes. Her shoulder bag was heavy with
guide books, maps, and the German phrase book she
had been trying to study on the plane.

*If you can't speak a language properly don't
speak it at all.* That was Kim's view. Sharon knew
that it was polite to try, that Germans, French people, Italians liked you to at least say, *Good morning,
I'd like a room with a shower, please,* in their language even if you couldn't respond to the next thing
they said.

They had spent two exhausting days looking at buildings restored after the war, at places where ancient monuments had stood long ago. And this morning, telling the tour guide they were going off on their own, had followed some people down a street and found themselves beside Marlene Dietrich's grave.

"I've only seen two of her movies," Kim said, sorrow in her voice.

Kim was quickly overwhelmed by strangeness, by beggars, street vendors, signs in foreign script, and needed help with everything from changing money to choosing her food. Growing up in a small Muskoka town was no excuse. Any person with a little wit could surely read a menu in a language with the same alphabet. And anyone knew that taking on the sorrows of a place could easily ruin a vacation.

"I wish we could have gone to Dubrovnik," she said for the fourth time.

Sharon closed her eyes and asked God for patience. If He was anywhere, He was surely here among the dead. There was Frankfurt yet to come and a side trip to a Bavarian castle, and Kim was going to go on pining for Dubrovnik. Tomorrow in the beer halls of Munich, while all around her jolly people were singing cheerful songs and shouting *Prosit!* and banging their steins together, she would sigh for Sarajevo.

In Sharon's apartment back in December and January they had sat on late in the evenings, sharing a pizza. The brochures lying around them on the floor, on the table, offered them the world in bright colours. They had talked of walking the Silk Road with backpacks, strong shoes, and endurance. Glossy shots of temple bells and ancient gods lured them Eastward.

But they knew there was a limit. Oriental mystery was something they could never afford.

And Kim said these trips with her were the best thing in her life.

In February, the papers had said the fighting would soon be over. Peacekeepers were on their way to Yugoslavia. It would be fine. A bargain price. The country needed tourist dollars. They would, by going there, be doing the Yugoslavs a favour. They booked the trip in a shared glow of altruism. Sitting side by side on the couch, they had drunk red wine and imagined themselves beside the Adriatic sea.

But in March and April old cities in flames lit up the TV screen. Pictures of anguished men carrying their friends through streets on stretchers were on page three of the newspaper every single day. Children cried for lost toys. Parents wept.

History got in the way of things. Upset the plans of ordinary people. But sometimes it changed things for the better. Now they were able to look at all of Berlin, back together again like a couple remarried after a long separation.

"There will be hostile feelings," Kim had said before they set off. "No one likes it when a whole lot of poor relations suddenly turn up wanting food and money. There will be bad feelings."

"Not for us," Sharon had replied. And so far this had been true.

The cemetery where once spies might have met and dropped messages in the clefts of trees was a pleasant place. Others were stopping by the grave, and farther off, at other memorial stones, friends and relatives were pulling up weeds and laying flowers down and talking softly as if the dead might hear. It was like a scene from one of those art movies which Kim enjoyed and Sharon did not.

She and Kim were as different as chalk and cheese. So why had she let herself in for this yet again. On her own, she would by now have met a host of new people and had at least one romantic adventure. They did meet men. Men would want to meet them both later, to take them for drinks, but after an hour or so there would be a loss of interest. Kim would not respond to the chat of strangers, couldn't seem to reach out and say, "Is that so?" at the right moment. If she wanted to find her man-in-the-garden, Sharon knew she would have to ditch Kim and strike out on her own.

"Let's go," she said. A quick glance at the grave would have done for her. She could tell her mother she had seen it, mention it at the office, and they would say, Oh really! and that would be that.

But still Kim lingered there.

"She was good at what she did," Kim said.

And so am I, Sharon wanted to say, wondering where the meanness she heard in her mind had come from. *I'm good at what I do and no one's going to have a public funeral for me and heap floral tributes on my grave!* Only her family and Marie and Jess and Kim would care. And only her mother and Kim would cry for her.

They had met, she and Kim, four years ago, when Kim had emerged from a relationship she still wouldn't talk about and applied for a job with UVT. Sharon at the time had just thrown Don out of her place and his seven suits after him. "So much for older men," she had said but meant, *So much for men*, period. "That's what you get for going with a man nearly old enough to be your father!" So her mother said, her sisters said and even her older brother said, who until then had been kind. And Sharon had decided after that to take up travel.

"A woman travelling alone," her mother had also said, "is at the mercy of any creep who comes along. A woman travelling alone is a prey. Take that nice new girl from the office with you." (Mother's consciousness still slept: Any woman under forty was a girl to her.) Sharon had three more years of girlhood to endure, Kim, five.

And in some ways, Kim was a girl. She looked like one. She kept slim, more from worry than from not eating. Her hair was straight with not even a hint of artificial colour in it. She said she loved to travel. When she got home she described the cities and the things they had seen vividly as if every moment had been exciting. But during the trips, she remained in her back-home mode, wandered round their shared room at night, not sleeping, sometimes got sick.

She was crouching by the grave now as if she could see the rotting flesh which had begun to waste in life. At ninety-two there was bound to be a falling away, flesh from bones, life from mind.

Sharon got her camera out to take a picture of Kim bending over the grave but hesitated, not sure if it was right. Showing people at the office. *And this is Kim on vacation.* Would they laugh at her, her serious sad face? Her breasts were outlined in her pink jacket as she bent forward. They were perfect, small and fine. Sharon turned away and quickly pushed the camera back into its case.

At the office Kim worked well but kept being passed over. She did the wrong things. She had no idea how to play the promotion game. At the lake last fall, they had been invited by Marty, Head of Sales, to a kind of office party out of town. And while the lake lapped on stones and the sun beat down and the rest of them listened to Marty talk about market share and new initiatives, Kim had wandered off alone. A couple of hours later, glowing, happy, she had returned with a piece of contorted driftwood that looked like a tortured animal, its tail twisted, its mouth open in a scream—or a song. She had presented it to Sharon and then sat down beside her, her slim legs red from the sun.

So here they were standing by the grave of a woman so unlike both of them it was unreal. She was glamorous, she was famous world-wide, her legs were perfect, her profile a work of art. When she sang, the universe stopped to listen. And in an interview she had said, "I'm good at what I do. I'm disciplined." Kim was right. She was good at what she did. It got her further, that's all.

Marty, in an aside up at the lake, had told Sharon that Kim could not be promoted, because while she worked hard she didn't have the people-skills to move up in Personnel. And Personnel was where the opportunities were now. Sharon had felt a little glow of satisfaction, understanding that he was telling her this because she was trusted; she could advance to the next square, no penalties. But then she felt sad because she wanted Kim to have the best of things too. She arranged these trips so that Kim could have a good time. And then regretted it.

"I'm going to that cafe we passed on the way here.

I'm going to have chocolate cake and coffee topped with cream. You can stay here if you like."

Kim looked blank. It was like Venice when all that Italian art and history had overwhelmed her into a state of dumb passivity. She saw Kim staring at her across a table in Poitiers, in Madrid.

Finally she grabbed Kim's arm and said, "Let's get out of here."

Kim had tears in her eyes. There was a stillness about her. She was alone in a separate space. In that moment, Sharon was truly aware of Kim, as if one of the stone angels nearby had come to life and shone its light directly into her friend's mind. Kim wasn't crying for this woman who had lived for decades at the peak of fame and fortune. She wasn't crying either out of envy or for her own lost chances and plain life.

Sharon touched Kim's hand and said, "There's nothing we can do for the people in Sarajevo, Kim. We would need an army, a fortune, the force of nations. We're two tourists, that's all."

Kim turned to her and said, "Thank you."

Her face, wet, was lovely. Like a pink Lady of the Sorrows.

"She knew a lot of songs," Kim said. "A lot of the men who heard her sing died young."

And she began to sing. Actually there and then began softly to sing, "'See what the boys in the backroom will have. And tell them I sighed, tell them I cried.'"

Sharon wanted to turn and run. People were looking at them and might at any moment call the police or begin to throw stones. She heard a rising murmur and looked for the gate, the way they'd come in.

But from the corners of the cemetery, from stones

and trees, words and notes grew as if the birds themselves were adding to the chorus. People were drawing
closer like the menacing pilgrims she had seen in an
opera on TV.

"'Tell them I sighed, and tell them I cried. And tell
them I died of the same.'"

A student snatched at Kim's sleeve. She drew back.
But the boy smiled at her. Laughed. A woman reached
out and kissed her on both cheeks. A man came and
shook her hand. And all the time they kept on singing.

Kim, knowing none of the language, Kim the lousy
traveller was leading all these foreigners in song, like a
chorus-master. She shone. It was like that moment at
the lake when she had given Sharon the piece of driftwood. The others had looked at Kim then as if she had
special knowledge, had done the right, enviable thing.

*Tell them I cried. Tell them I sighed. AND TELL
THEM I DIED OF THE SAME!*

People were coming towards them with flowers,
with love, with tributes. A man in a brown hat put a
bunch of daisies into Sharon's arms. She was filled with
music. And Kim was outlined for her in a new light, a
light that might be everlasting, at least in this life. The
clear knowledge of wasted time made Sharon take hold
of her friend and fellow-traveller with both hands.

She turned Kim towards her and kissed her on the
mouth, and with their arms round each other they
stood there for a moment, alone in their new light. And
then they allowed the music back in. There was respectful applause.

"Next year we'll stay home," Sharon said as they
walked toward the gate.

"I'd like that," Kim replied.

"I'm owed two weeks."

"We'll get a place with a backyard."

There would be a garden, Sharon thought. There could be a tree against the wall. Apricots. "'Oh time stand still,'" she whispered to herself. And Kim, holding her hand, led her away, away from the place of the dead towards the cafe, into the heart of Berlin.

STANLEY

Myra watched Peter eating a slice of toast spread too thickly with jam and wondered how long she could keep quiet about the phone call. She opened her mouth to speak but Stanley yapped and Peter turned round to give him a crust.

The day that dog had entered the house, order went out of the window. It ate. It chewed. It relocated shoes and books and towels. After a week of watching it leaping up to try and catch the pendulum of the cuckoo clock, Peter had said, "That dog isn't right in the head."

"It's a puppy," Myra answered then, determined to be forbearing even though the house had taken on a different and not very clean smell. Kim had asked them to take it. It was a stray; she was out all day, and it wasn't fair to keep a dog in the city. He would be happier with them, she said. But Myra knew it was just another of her tricks to keep the old folks occupied and give them something to think about besides that grim harvester grinding its way towards them with its arms of steel, gathering up those who were ready as well as those who weren't.

"Crazy, a dog at our age," Peter said. "Eh, Sir Stanley." And the dog answered with a puppy's sharp voice, demanding attention again.

He'd christened it Stanley after Sir Stanley Mathews who was said to be living in Toronto and not well off. Sports players hadn't earned the kind of money in his day that they did now. None of them got to be millionaires and drive fancy cars. You didn't see their faces on billboards then. They played for the sake of the game, for the team and, if they were exceptional, for their country. Now everybody who could kick or catch or hit a ball only wanted to get rich.

Listening to him, drinking her coffee, Myra tried to remember what had once been so romantic about their love. She wanted to shout at him across the table and make him tell her why he'd done something so crazy as to start betting his pension money on a game. But Kim was on her way and wouldn't want to find them arguing. It was possibly a safe bet. The papers were backing Azurri. But all the same he'd no right to go throwing money away without telling her.

The World Cup being played on the same continent was no excuse. Though she could see he enjoyed it. He complained that the commentators talked out of the sides of their mouths and a lot of the rules had changed, but he followed every move, shouted at the players, insulted the referee from the safety of his armchair. It was like a renewal of life for him. There was youth in his face again, something of the old excitement.

Those few years he'd stayed on in England after the war, before they were married, he'd gone every Saturday to watch Blackpool play, arguing the rest of the week with her father about missed goals. Every Monday, he'd filled out his coupon, mailed it and then waited five days for a fortune. All he'd ever won was three shillings and sixpence in the old money. Saturday evening on the wireless: Plymouth Northend, nil—Sheffield Wednesday, two; Liverpool, three—Bristol Rovers, one; Partick Thistle, one—Hamilton Academicals, nil. That plummy voice could destroy a million dreams of wealth in the ten minutes it took to go through the list.

Soccer, though he never said, was what he'd liked most about England. He'd never got used to the weather or the coffee. She'd sometimes thought it was the coffee that drove him to return home to Canada and take her with him.

She knew he'd thought once or twice of going to seek out his hero in Toronto but had never done so, maybe not wanting to see the player who'd scored so many brilliant goals turned into a tired old man.

Hockey had somehow never caught on with him, so in his retirement he spent winter evenings reading and planning his vegetable beds. The last weekend in May, he'd be out in the backyard, planting and weeding. And now there was Stanley to dig up the bulbs and bury bones in the lawn. Peter picked the dog up and rubbed his face on its furry back and Myra imagined fleas hopping off onto his beard and then into their bed and so onto her, and their lives becoming one long scratch. But she only said, "The grandchildren will like it. If we ever have any."

It was a fine day for the drive from Toronto. Myra wished she'd planned a cold meal, chicken and two kinds of salad. But ham and scalloped potatoes were easy. And she'd try for a moment alone with Kim. Kim, though, had her own troubles. There she was, thirty-seven, in an only all right job that some might see as a dead end. Single and childless and still sharing that little house with another woman. Myra peeled the broccoli stalks so she could put them in, cut small, with the rest. At times, she wondered how Kim stayed so cheerful. And had told her she'd never meet a man if she went about all the time with Sharon. She sprinkled salt lightly over the vegetables and felt guilty doing it. They were all afraid of salt now. And butter. And eggs. But generations had grown up eating all those things and were none the worse for it. There was nothing wrong with Sharon really but she was over forty and not pretty by any stretch.

Last time she'd told Kim to go out on her own more, she'd seen Kim's eyes fill with tears so had stopped and had made a resolution not to mention it again if she could help it. Whenever Thea's grandchildren came over from next door, Myra caught herself hoping they wouldn't grow too fast but would be playmates for Kim's little ones. She had patterns hidden away for dresses and bonnets and outfits she might knit one day in pink or blue for Kim's babies. Though these days you saw toddlers dressed in mad colours like purple and black as if parents didn't care what their offspring looked like. Her own mother had always dressed the two of them alike, her and Kate, in flowered gingham frocks till Kate got thinner and taller and began to complain.

The cuckoo squawked. Time to put the pies in. Crust waited for no man. Four pies all made with Peter's harvest of rhubarb. No point in making only one pie.

There was always a use for pies: A sudden potluck supper. The "girls'" Friday bridge. A family newly bereaved.

When a man, reliable for forty years except for one small lapse, turns to gambling, something is wrong, she would say to Kim. Intensely and deeply wrong. Whatever he'd bet on the game was bound to be more than they could afford and there was no telling where it might end. Drawing money too soon from their retirement plans. Disappearing to Las Vegas. Taking up with thin blondes.

After HER death, after Marlene Dietrich died two years ago, a little while after, Peter had begun to walk freer, as if she'd carried off a whole lot of bad war memories to be buried with her in Germany. The change had been all to the good. He'd become more talkative. Taken notice of things. And now he'd gone too far. Putting money on eleven men in little shorts kicking a ball about.

"Stanley!"

He was out there petting the dog and trying to get the silly, hairy creature to move the ball with its front paws.

She heard the car drive up and went out gladly, only drawing back a bit when Sharon got out of the car first and came towards her with that hopeful smile. She was tall and her hair was cut straight, though a little curl wouldn't have done any harm. She walked with her face turned up slightly, defiant. *Hello Myra. Hi there, Sharon.*

Kim behind her was carrying the flowers. They always brought flowers from the city to the country. She wanted to tell them that she didn't need gifts and certainly not flowers at this time of year, but there was no decent way of saying anything except "Thank you, these are lovely, I'll put them in water."

Sharon went through into the garden and Kim followed Myra into the kitchen. For a moment, through the window, they watched Sharon giving Stanley a hug and taking his ball and throwing it towards the beans and the dog dancing after it.

"If the game goes to extra time, we'll eat off trays," Myra said. "Tell me how you are, Kimmie." And she began cutting the ends off the carnations and daisies.

"We're taking inventory. It's driving everybody crazy."

"Counting everything?"

"We do it on computer, Mum."

Myra had figured that out but didn't say. Everything was on computer now and she couldn't see that it was for the better. She knew all about PCs and e-mail and the 'net too. But you had to let the young think they had the edge. A lot of people assumed that ignorance came with age, that senior minds hung a sign up, Gone fishing! And used to being taken for idiots, older folk often said nothing when they could have taught the young ones a thing or two.

"It's nice to see you, love." Myra paused, trying not to ask the next question, but it came out of its own accord. "Have you been out lately?"

"We've seen a couple of new plays," Kim answered sharply. "The pies smell good."

"I've thought of getting a smaller stove. Just the two of us. But I like to bake." Myra knew she said that every time but couldn't help repeating it. It was a safe thing to say.

Both of them looked at the old double oven. Ham in

one, pies in the other. The potatoes would go in after half time.

"Who do you think's going to win, Mom?"

Myra told her about the bet sooner than she'd intended, how she'd overheard the phone call and then worried about it through the night.

"It's as if I didn't know your father. After all these years."

"Who does anyone know, really," Kim said. "Do you know me?"

Myra put her knife down too stunned to speak. The kitchen walls closed in. A door slammed shut. You're my daughter! she wanted to shriek out, top-voiced, bringing Thea round from next door to see what was wrong. My daughter who I dressed and fed and took to school and loved and cried over and still want happiness for. Still want contentment, love, a family for.

Before she could think of an answer to speak out loud, Sharon came in from the garden with the dog in her arms.

"The game starts in five minutes," she said.

She held Stanley out to Kim like a kind of holy offering, looking at Kim, holding her eyes in a way Myra could only recall from long ago. Kim looked back at Sharon, couldn't stop herself. And reached for the animal, touching Sharon's hands as she took hold of him.

There was an electric feeling in the kitchen as if sparks had been set alight and were dancing in the air. Myra ran out to the backyard, afraid.

Pictures flashed into her head: A little girl crying because she had to wear a pretty dress to a party instead of jeans; an older girl sitting up in a tree on her own; a daughter older still coming home quiet and unhappy from the school dance. And a picture of Kim and Sharon together that she couldn't bear to hold in her mind.

Peter was tying up the pepper plants, knotting twine round the thin stalks. Myra looked at him. He looked at her. Saw her face. Looked past her through the kitchen window. Then he set his cutters down and his ball of string and put his arms round her. The sleeves of his shirt were grimy, but she didn't draw back.

"They'll be all right," he said.

After a long time, she answered him.

"There seems to be love," she said.

"I think I've known for a while."

"You never said."

"Best for you to find out in your own good time."

"Is it our fault?"

"I don't think there's a fault there," he answered. "No cause for blame."

Everything was changing. He hadn't held her like that for months. And now, with this new knowledge, he wasn't numb with shock. It was all plain to him, as if he was the wise one, as if he had, all on his own, acquired a way of looking at things that was specially his.

She wanted to ask how this had come about but knew he couldn't have answered. It was only to do with being older, with looking at things from a distance and seeing what mattered and what didn't. And perhaps too it had something to do with his dead idol, even maybe with the dog.

"Let's go in," he said. "I've got two hundred dollars on the game."

"Peter!"

"If I win, I'll take you to that place in Toronto. You can buy a new coat. We need a new rug for the bedroom."

She drew back from him.

He went on, "I fancied a bit of a flutter, that's all. A last chance at a fortune."

"You put it on the Italians? On Azurri?"

"No," he said. "Brazil. I like their looks. The odds are better. Ravelli's a good man."

"It's a lot of money."

"We'll go to Toronto anyway, win or lose. Perhaps stay over night. Kim's asked us many a time."

She was about to say the kind of thing she had often said: Toronto! Who needs to go there. There's everything we need here in Winouski. Toronto's noisy and dirty and dangerous besides.

Peter said, "If you'd like to, that is." And he stood there waiting, as if the game couldn't begin till she answered yes or no.

Like to? For years now, it seemed, she hadn't thought of anything but getting on with day-to-day life. Her meetings. The shopping. Cooking. Keeping the place clean, polishing the old table and chairs, doing the laundry. She did all these things like a ritual, with care and in the right order, to ward off the perils of old age. As if, in the very act of stopping or doing one thing instead of another on a certain day, she would invite disaster in the shape of a stroke, a heart attack, or death itself.

There was a smell of cut grass in the air. Everything around them was green. The tomato plants, the peppers. Beans. With a little care and sun and water, they sprang out of the ground and flourished.

"I would like a coat," she replied. "Dark blue maybe. One of those lightweight ones. And while we're there, I'll get some wool. When winter comes, that dog'll be needing a jacket."

THE
DAY
MARLENE
DIETRICH
DIED

On the day Marlene Dietrich died, Richard Mawson left the cottage near Grenoble and set out to visit his mother in Sussex. He locked the white front door and trailed his hand over the flowers by the wall, inhaling a mixture of herbs and young roses. His work could wait. And so could the new waitress in the bistro. She had slim legs and vermilion hair and the other day he had said to her, "That park over there is the place for lovers. It inspired a great writer to write his masterpiece."

You are out of your mind! Words of his first wife, she of the limited vocabulary. Years ago, standing in the Louvre, she had said that to him. People had stared. She had said it loud and often, about his work, his life, his choice of music, the clothes he wore.

You're crazy! The voice of Ellen, his second. Fewer words. But she had preferred Bob Dylan.

In chorus they would have told him it was madness to set off on this trip now with four weeks of steady work still to be done on his book just because a woman he had supposed immortal was dead.

The car that came with the cottage was an old Peugeot and it ran like a dream. *Use it, use it*, the Duvaliers had said, thinking of local errands only. He had decided to drive to Paris and fly from there. He could visit the Louvre on his way back and treat himself to the violent colours of the nineteenth century before plunging into the cold stone and marble of antiquity. And the journey would give him time to think about a new title for his manuscript. *The Effects of Wartime Song Lyrics on Current Gender Politics* was five words too long.

His mother's name was Frances but for years she had called herself Francine. She was seventy-one-and-a-half and could well be cracking up from the arthritis she had been mentioning intermittently for twenty years. As for her heart, the gesture of hand on chest as if to show him that yes, indeed, she had a heart and all the pain in it was caused by him, came to his mind with awful clarity. That heart might even now be beating slowly and more slowly day by day, threatening to stop. Her eyes too were getting weaker. *I have an appointment with the optometrist. Just stronger lenses, darling.*

Blindly she was moving into the area of easy accidents. Stairwells, lift shafts, heavy traffic; deathtraps all. The phone call would come. *Your mother is asking for you.* Summoned by proxy.

He hadn't seen her since the last quarrel three years ago. He had phoned now and then, a cool and dutiful son. The sound of duty in his voice brought out reproach in hers. She wasn't going to start now apologising for her lovers, for the times in his childhood she had said, "Go out to play, Richard, sweetheart," and locked the door behind him. And that argument had ended like all the others with her telling him to buy a decent suit and grow up and him shouting back, "I'm thirty-seven, Mother!"

He stopped in a little place near Lyon for lunch, steak à cheval and a bottle of red, and then drove on with Marlene singing for him, *I'm warm again, in love again.* She sat there on a barrel showing her suspenders and sang, *Ich bin die fesche Lola.*

He sang along with her and didn't notice the curve till he was in it and the stone wall loomed up in front of him, and then he screamed out in fear. "Marlene! Mother!! Mummy!"

Blackness. Awakening. And then as he struggled out of the car and examined its dented front, its battered side, he kicked it, felt fury rise up; touched his head, saw blood on his hand, wanted to scream again.

The gendarmes were for once sympathetic. So monsieur was really used to the roads? Just a little wine for lunch? Regular two-month stay in their lovely country to do research and to write? Interesting! They advised him, after keeping him in a steamy office for three hours, to get a taxi back to Lyon and from there take the TGV. No doubt the insurance company would pay for the damage to the car. The problem could be settled on his return. A man on his way to see his sick and aging mother. Eh bien. The train would be leaving at eight p.m.

The younger policeman smiled at him with the smile of a ruler who had charge over all his comings and goings and who knew that his mother was a young woman of twenty-nine who had long legs and who would welcome him at the door, naked, a maenad.

Richard wanted to lash out, to bash the young confident face, mark it with his knuckles, draw blood. He stood outside the gendarmerie, his back against the wall till his breath returned to normal and his fists unclenched.

I could have died.

At the station in Lyon they told him that there was no seat on a train to Paris till midnight. Summer crowds, monsieur. Already here in May. Les touristes! Other more hostile invasions had been less unpopular.

He tried to change his plans and fly from Lyon but the planes too were fully booked. You have a plane ticket from Paris, monsieur! He looked up at the hazy sky for a sign that would tell him to stay with the Duvaliers' Peugeot, wait till it was repaired, to turn round and go back to his cottage and the new waitress and forget England.

The woman who came up to him and offered him her body was not slim, did not have good legs nor a fine complexion. She had a slight lisp and was wearing a sweater too tight and a skirt too short. And she was hungry. After dinner he took her to his room and made love to her unkindly. Later on, she agreed to go with him for a gentle walk beside the river. She talked about her life as it had been once and mentioned that she had a son aged five whom she saw off to school every morning.

"See his picture. I call him René. But I wish I'd called him something better, a solid name like Richard. Perhaps when he grows up, he'll be a writer like you."

The trees bent over the river, branches sweeping the surface. When he put his hands on her shoulders she turned to him and smiled. He had not thought to fill the pockets of her coat with stones. The branches swished to and fro brushing the water violently. And her face as she looked back at him was wet.

On the train his fellow passenger turned to talk to him. "You're from where?"

"Manchester."

"What do you do?"

They always asked because his French was not perfect and he was too young to have given up another life to spend declining years in one place.

"I'm a singer," he told her, tired for once of truth.

"Marlene Dietrich died yesterday," she said.

He wanted to say, *What's it to you! What does it matter to you? Who are you that you can use her name in that familiar way?*

But she went on, "We're using the same currency now. That has to count for something."

He bit into the white hard baguette and crumbs spilled down from his mouth. Everybody was an expert. Everybody knew everything. Information technology. Universal access. At the university, other lecturers blamed the telly for slack work, for poor perceptions when it was their own lack of imagination that made students into zombies.

He laughed at the others in his department. He knew they laughed at him. They tittered and muttered about his research. If he had been scouring graveyards, battlefields, searching for wounds and old bones, they would have taken him seriously. When they heard sounds of singing coming from his office, voices of Vera and Frank and Bing, the jokes of Bob Hope, they shook their heads and went back to their boring searches into the current political soul. They saw his work as a poor excuse for scholarship, his clothes as affectation, and his desire for solitude as a symptom of madness.

When he had mentioned Grenoble to the new lecturer in Economics, she, smiling, had turned her neat face to him in academic complicity and said, "Ah Stendhal!" and waited for a loving response. When he replied, "George Formby!" she had moved away to join the others.

He went to the St. Jacques near the Jardin des Plantes where he usually stayed in Paris and took a room for the night.

In the hotel lobby a woman sat crying. Her name was Carla.

"You can't understand," she said. "You can't know what I feel."

"I'm on my way to have breakfast."

"Do you think I want to eat." She turned on him, angry, full of horror at his lack of understanding. "Coffee perhaps. Give me time to change."

He phoned to let his mother know that he was approaching and would be there the next day late or, at any rate, the day after.

His mother, in a quavery voice, said, "Did you know Marlene Dietrich died yesterday? I remember her saying in that documentary somebody made, 'I've been photographed to death.'"

It wasn't the camera that killed her, Mother! She was old, like you.

Carla, when she returned, had dried her tears, was wearing purple, a scarf tied round her neck in that neat foreign way, colours of green and blue and black and turquoise.

"How do you tie your scarf?"

"Like a man's tie."

She fingered the knot as she sat there talking.

"They said she couldn't walk, never went out. But she did, she went out every day. Every day about this time, she went by the boulangerie on the corner, the one over there. About this time. She bought three croissants which made me think she was not alone. No one could eat three croissants for breakfast, and theirs are particularly large. See. See. There she is. Buying her croissants. She is not dead."

She pointed and he looked and saw an old bent woman with a scarf on her head and her raincoat collar turned up, wearing boots and carrying a plastic bag. Not a single feature could be seen. Not a glimmer of fame or riches and no retinue of wishful men to walk behind her. This old lady had not danced and sung her way through his life. Had not made movies that were old when he was young.

"Let's go for a walk," he said to Carla.

"What about—you know."

"Later if there's time."

He took her to the cemetery to see where the grave might have been had Marlene wished to be buried there. And he said, "She is dead. Dead. And will be taken back to Germany."

"Why there?"

"She wanted to be near her mother."

"What about her lovers?"

He saw a long grave, suffocated in flowers, a grave stretching half across Paris, a grave in which the bodies of her old lovers lay. Exhumed and sent from Hollywood, from London, from Berlin, from Sicily, and laid beside her, facing her. *I'm warm again. In love again.*

"Why have you brought me here?"

"Why do people go anywhere?"

He put his hands on the scarf, on her chest. She thought it must be time and said, "Not here."

But he replied, "No better place," and pulled and pulled on the knot of the scarf she had tied for him in advance and afterwards left her there while she was still faintly gasping.

He picked up his bag from the hotel and took the bus to Charles de Gaulle and paid the fee to take an earlier flight.

Even three years ago, his mother had begun to stoop; her hair was by now thin on top and her face probably like a parchment, dried and full of wrinkles. "I will love you. I will be your only love," he murmured to himself and sang "Lili Marlene" under his breath and wished for lamplight and the soft glow of gas mantles. Everywhere nowadays light was harsh. Neon made much of life into a B-movie.

They were slow in the car rental office at Gatwick. He wanted to bang on the desk and shout, This is my home. I'm on my way to see my mother. She is old, maybe dying. Minutes count. GIVE ME A CAR! Finally the young man handed him a set of keys and released him.

He drove slowly south into the rolling countryside. The trees were heavy with leaves, the grass lush, the sun soft and unthreatening.

I'm on my way, Mother.

He could stay in his old room for the rest of the summer, live with her, take care of her, do his research in the library, ask her to sing the songs she had sung then, as she went from camp to camp with ENSA in the war. *The best time of my life, sweetheart. Before you were born.*

The house was still there. He felt a sense of relief as

if it might have disappeared and left a gap in the road, as if the shrubs, dull evergreens planted by his father years before—*your father came to like darkness in the war*—might have grown over the place. But it was there, the house. It reached out to him. The windows glowed clean; the outside light was on as if she had left it on all these years to await his return. It was daylight and the outside light was on! Inside him the anger softened. *Save electricity! Do you think I'm made of money?* had been one of his father's cries. And now his mother had left the light on overnight perhaps and maybe for days, just for him, for his return.

He walked up the path—the hedge needed cutting, well, he would cut the hedge—and saw himself:

Walking down that path behind his father's coffin.

Walking down that path, bride on his arm.

Walking down that path with his new bicycle.

Walking down that path with his new bride.

Walking down that path alone with his suitcase.

You do not need to go to Manchester, his mother had called after him as if there were jobs available everywhere and he had taken that one for spite.

She was there inside.

He looked through the window and watched his mother. She was setting out two places on the table. She had put a starched place mat at either end, lacy heirlooms from a time when people knew how to starch lightly, how to iron without ripping lacework to shreds. In the centre of the table, more highly polished than he had remembered it, was a single red rose in a light vase, its stem showing through the glass. She was in the act of laying down a silver knife when she looked up and saw him. And he was staring at her and thinking this is my home, this is my mother and I forgive her. This is my home, this is my mother and.

His mother came to the door and said, "Oh dear, did I leave that light on again. I'm getting very forgetful."

She came to him smiling and put her hands on his cheeks, just in the way he remembered. And she said, "How lovely to see you, sweetheart. You're looking well. Over there agrees with you. What a surprise. Why didn't you let me know the exact time?"

She looked slimmer, was wearing a brown skirt, a blouse in shades of pink, high-heeled shoes that set off her slim legs, and her hair was tinted a rosy beige.

Still she was his mother and he could forgive her.

"What a nice surprise," she said.

He beheld her. She looked very, very well. She smelt lightly of *Carnation*. He had made this journey assuming she would be tottering, perhaps close to death. And now here she was, looking as if she was on the very verge of life. For several moments, he had no words to say. He would stay on and take her to London every day to theatres, to galleries. Make up for time and love lost. Hand in hand, they would go and have great times and he would listen again to her wartime stories and the old tale of her lost lover. And she would sing to him, sing the old sad songs to him of soldiers gone to war and of the women waiting at home for them in vain.

She said, "Darling. Put your bag in your old room. You don't want to be spending your time with dreary old me. I'm sure you want to see your friends. There's a train to Victoria at one. You've got a car? Just come and go as you like."

He said, "I've come all this way to see you."

"Angel, how sweet."

And then she said, "The pub serves a very good smoked trout."

She smiled at him slyly just in the way he remembered.

"But you and me," she went on, "we'll have a lovely, cosy dinner tonight or maybe tomorrow."

"Yes, Mother."

He carried his bag back outside. She, uncorking a bottle of wine, did not notice. He thought he heard her singing. He thought he heard her singing the song she had often sung to him. *Ich bin von Kopf bis Fuss auf Liebe eingestellt.* And he remembered how she would tap his head and then his feet and repeat the line again. Liebchen, she would say. My little love.

Richard had liked it better when she sang fast and loud, *I am the naughty Lola*, and turned on the piano stool and swung her legs at him and laughed. And they had both laughed.

I can't help it. It's my nature.

He put his case in the car and walked to the Green. There was no one about. It was lunchtime. Everybody was at home or in the pub.

He sat down by the pond to watch the swans, and when a young woman, blue suit, nice eyes, thick ankles, sat down on the same bench to feed the birds and offered him a crust, he accepted it gratefully.

Soon he would say to her, *Robert Louis Stevenson lived near here, and if we walk up on the Downs just a little way we can see the place that inspired him to write his third novel.*

And she would follow him, the literary man, and discover too late that his true interest was in the songs of the Second World War.

IN
MEMORIAM

"Darling," she said.

He said, "I heard on the radio."

She put her nose into the bouquet of carnations and babies'-breath and ferns and sniffed them as if they were the first flowers anyone had ever given her. She looked across at him and smiled showing bright teeth, but there were tears on her cheeks.

"For a corpse?"

"You sing her songs."

"What are you saying?"

He reached across the table and grasped her hand because he wasn't sure what he was saying. Meaning was of no interest to him. He only wanted her to step down off her stage, the stage she made out of every floor she walked on, every room she entered, and make him secure.

"I love you."

"What shall we have?"

"I'm sorry that she's gone," he lied.

She accepted his sorrow. Turning her face, she as-

sumed for a moment the haughty expression of the
dead star. He wanted to shake her by the shoulders till
the mask fell away. But she turned her head to the light
and said huskily, "How can I help but cry for her?"

The dress she was wearing caught points of light, a
harsh covering over soft silk underwear.

"Are you wearing the green?"

She nodded. He wanted to pull her under the table
and fuck her right there while the waiter brought their
food and said will there be anything else, sir? as they
moaned and she cried out yesyesyes.

If it had been a saintly woman, a good woman,
Moira wept for, he might have understood. But that
free-wheeling Lola who had run amok among swaths
of men and women and left their husks to rot! Was she
worth tears?

He hated the dining room with its posters and lyrics of songs used as wallpaper, and signed photographs
of stars who had eaten their stroganoff here. He liked
classic restaurants with panelling and discreet lighting
and hidden corners. Moira, cheerful again, was pick-
ing out slim options from the menu.

"Darling," she said. "Let's have the fish, grilled. And
share a salad."

"I'm having liver," he answered. "It's the only good
thing here."

The waiter took their order and backed away, keeping his eyes on Moira as long as he could without falling into the salad bar.

"What have you done today?"

Moved a mountain! Stayed a river in its course,
slain a dragon, wrestled a bear to the ground. What do
you think I've done, my love?

"First thing, I told Jackson what he could do with his contract. Went over the papers for the Emerald account. They want a sixteen-day holdover. I'm going to say no."

She watched him as if every word made sense to her. But at the back of her mind, he knew, a different libretto played. He let himself smile. After all, she was there. She was there with him, Tom, in Toronto with its unique penile symbol, its familiar shapes, its gold towers. She wasn't going to New York for weeks. Chicago was two months away.

He said, "The threat of separation is making the market nervous."

"They'll get used to it."

"And you?" he asked. "What have you done?"

"Bernie came round and we played duets. Then I rehearsed for Sunday. I've changed the program. It will be all Dietrich. A kind of in memoriam. You'll be there?"

Of course he would be there. It meant much to her that he sat in that seat, front row centre, never taking his eyes off the stage. In the intermission when he hurried to the dressing room to tell her she was better than ever, she always smiled that brilliant smile at him before she turned back to her mirror. And sometimes she reached for his hand, a child seeking reassurance. She did so now across the table. And the figment of a man called Norbert who might await her in New York dissolved. In Chicago, a conceivable Charles fell unremarked down an elevator shaft.

In bed in the Bay Street apartment, she was all his. His mind danced around this. It was fact. Real. And tomorrow in the money market, stocks would also rise.

Foreigners, two women and a man, stopped by their table, looking down, pleased to be seen with her, pleased that she talked to them.

"We're sorry," they said as if the dead woman were a family member known to them all. *Suddenly gone and sorely missed.*

"Danke schön."

It irked him that Moira could speak languages of which he knew only the words for hello and goodbye and please show me the way to the church. When she talked to these interlopers, these strangers, there was that warmth in her voice which he loved and which he wished she would use only to him.

His mother had said to him over and over, why do you always choose to do what is difficult? As if he climbed impossible rocks or spent his weekends on his hands and knees in underground caves seeking new depths. She had never understood that he wanted nothing ordinary.

On Thursdays, after his meeting with the partners, he had lunch with his mother at the Green Parrot. Never nowadays at her comfortable club. She had gone in for healthy eating and didn't believe it was available at any restaurant with clean white tablecloths and well-dressed waiters. Over gritty lentil soup and a chunk of brown bread like a doorstop, she looked at him, concerned, as if he might have lost all his hair or turned yellow with hepatitis in the night.

She said, "Have you been to the doctor's lately?"

"I'm fine, Mother."

"You always say that."

"Because it's true."

She shook her head and all the thoughts in that

head, at least the ones regarding him, were apparent between them: You could have made a good marriage; worked harder; lived closer to me; she is for everyone; you're neglecting your own life; your old age will be lonely; you have no children; a different kind of man could cope with her but you need someone gentle and warm who would be kind—to me.

"And how does Moira feel now that her model has died?"

"She has songs of her own, Mother."

"It will affect her, you know. Marlene was an icon for many."

In spite of her dislike, she had time for the feelings of the other woman, and he heard the warning in her voice. It irritated him beyond reason that his own mother could also sympathise with Moira and with the old woman who was now, and not before time, dead.

He refused dessert and said sharply that he had to get to work. After a morning away, there was much to do.

At the office they cried out, rushing at him like cooing birds, "Marlene is going to be buried in Berlin." As if they had any of them been old enough to see her or go to her concerts or care about the quality of the prints of old movies.

He simply replied, because wit was expected of him in that place, "So the Blue Angel is a true angel at last."

And they laughed. Because it was funny? Or because he was their boss? He didn't care. It was part of a ritual.

Donna, the new accountant who never got his jokes, said, "The Blue Angel was a club. It wasn't her."

The afternoon dragged.

That night in bed Moira was all his again, and he knew that he was not the passenger in her life but the driver. She cried out and it was entirely for him. That was the knowledge that kept him sane when he saw her in the recording studio fawned on by the producer, the engineers. When women who wanted to catch the infection of her borrowed glamour bent down to her in restaurants. When flowers arrived, sent by men whose names he did not know.

On Friday, he got home early. The market was stable. Nothing would happen till early next week. From the hall he heard no sound and imagined her poised over her music. He loved it when she performed for him, only for him, in their own private place. He would creep in and pour wine into two fragile glasses and ask her to sing a love song from an earlier time.

He opened the door softly. She wasn't alone. He could see two heads above the piano top, close, whispering. She and Bernadette were at the piano, side by side on the bench. They weren't playing. There were no notes. Only a soft murmuring sound. He coughed. Moira turned and then thumped her fist down on the keys. They began to play loudly, the mocking intro to a song he'd never heard. And then, turning, they did a double bow as if they were dressed for performance in glossy black gowns and he were an audience of thousands.

Bernie always wore, for practice, T-shirts cut low at the front, leotards tight over her pulpy thighs. She bent down to pick up her music case.

Moira said, "You're home early sweetheart."

"I'll be on my way," Bernie said pushing music into her case. "See you tomorrow, honey."

She pecked Tom's cheek as she went by him. Moira turned and waved to her and then smiled at him.

The door closed.

"I'll get the wine," he said.

"Juice for me, darling."

Her face was flushed.

Next morning Moira said, "You're not eating your toast, sweetheart."

"Thinking about you. About tonight. About later."

"Tonight? I'm at Bernie's till late. We have to practise. If we practise there, then we don't disturb you."

"You practise all day."

"This is a very important concert. Now that she's died, we have to choose the songs with care. We have to get the flavour right."

"And after, next week, you'll sing songs of your own?"

"You've never liked her."

That was ridiculous but he didn't say so. How could he either not like or like someone so remote from him, someone only known through photographs and lines of songs.

You say auf wiedersehen but you mean good riddance.

Men swarm around me like flies and if they burn, I'm not to blame.

"You sing her songs," he said.

"I wear her kind of clothes," she responded. "But I am me, sweetheart. Bernie is writing something new and different for me. You'll love it."

That night at dinner she talked about the funeral, Marlene's final homecoming.

"I thought of going but you know, it's more important to stay and sing. The concert's almost sold out."

Who were they, the people who came to listen to songs that harked back to an old professor in a chicken suit, to a war and the memory of hundreds and thousands of dead people? They couldn't all be old soldiers, old veterans of both sexes who had been thrilled to see her amongst them, brightening their days off from the slaughter. Most of them would be nostalgia junkies, happy to pay twenty-five dollars and more to wallow in the past of others.

"Coffee?"

"No thanks. You know what it does to my voice."

"I'll drive you over there."

"You're tired sweetheart. I've called a cab."

She left and he sat in the armchair to read his thoughts alone. It crossed his mind that many men in his position would have gone after other women. But he had not, in the seven years of their relationship, considered that option. Even when she was away for six weeks at a time. He saw himself as devoted, a word he liked and never considered pejorative. There was nothing dog-like in his constancy. He was a hero in ancient stories wading through blood and decades to get to his true love.

The phone rang. His mother wanted to talk. Her sister had called and it must be, she said, two o'clock in the morning over there. He held the receiver away from his ear. He didn't want to hear what his cousin Richard had done now. "Came and went," his mother said. "Said hello and left." It was no help to say that he was crazy or to remind her of the time Richard had threatened to bite his ear off. He said he was sorry and goodnight and went back to his own thoughts.

When he said to people, "Moira is devoted to music," the images in his head were of votaries and vestal virgins carrying lighted candles towards an altar. "I am devoted," he said aloud, and looked at the pictures of naked women in the book on his knees, full figures painted in the eighteenth century. The little gold clock on the bookshelf said it was half past eleven. Near midnight.

I've come to fetch you home, darling?

Why not? She would only have to call a taxi otherwise. Taxis could be dangerous. And in any case it was late. The night before the concert she needed rest. And he wanted her, wanted her, would die before morning if he couldn't hold her warm in his arms.

He went down to the Stygian cave to get his car. It was the kind of place where in movies the bad guys lurked with submachine guns. But he with loving purpose was guarded from harm. He knew that.

She would be surprised to see him, would love him more. They would drink wine and talk and make love, and she would sleep all day tomorrow while he tidied the apartment and went shopping for groceries and wine.

Backing out of the garage he nearly ran down a cat which leapt out of the way, its mouth shaped square in an indignant howl.

He parked outside Bernadette's house and saw the light on in the front room. He waited, looking up at the windows. Half an hour passed. Two cops stopped by to look in the car window. He told them he had come to fetch Moira Horoka, the singer. They gave the car a respectful look and walked on. Ready to shoot. Ready to kill. Happy to protect.

It seemed to grow darker although the street lights were still on and the moon hadn't changed. He walked up the steps and rang the bell. Bernadette opened the door and led him to the living room.

"Darling, you're up late," Moira said.

"I came to fetch you."

"I was planning to stay the night."

Bernadette smiled cat-like, looking from one to the other.

Moira was wearing a silk robe.

"I was getting ready for bed. But now you're here."

He stood there smiling, but in his mind he ran to a dark place. Ran out of the room, down a street to a bridge, any bridge. He ran from the room, down the street onto the bridge and leaned there in the rain, able to cry because rain covered tears. He grasped the railing and looked at the water or the railway line that ran below.

Fearing the rushing train or ice-cold river less than his new fear of her, he jumped and would not be saved.

Dragging her with him, he rushed again to the bridge and this time pushed her onto the roof of the fast train as it sped by beneath.

Moira returned to them wearing her jeans and thin shirt.

Tom tried to close the door for the time being on the scene in his head and said goodbye politely to Bernadette.

"When you sing someone else's songs," Moira said as he drove her back to the apartment, "you can't help being a little like them."

"I understand," he said. But he didn't understand and he never would.

He dropped her off at the front door, watched her safely into the foyer, and drove down into the garage. As he guided the car into its particular space in that dark cavern, he knew what it was that made for danger there. He knew the kind of men who lurked underground waiting to commit terrible deeds.

He cried real tears. Mourning the dead woman at last. Mourning his own devotion. Weeping for the weakness that had kept him devoted, in his front row seat, leading the applause. He wept in dread of the dark place that had opened up in his mind, a place he had kept hidden till now, even from himself.

HI!
MY
NAME
IS
HAROLD
FRYER

When Harold Fryer went to church that Sunday, he had to begin by reminding God of his existence. As a boy he had sung "Jesus loves me" often enough to believe he was known up there in the sky among the clouds and angels. Once, when he was about eleven, he had seen a vision of the Christ Child in colour on his bedroom wall. But at twelve he had lost religion and learnt to blow frogs apart with firecrackers. Now, thirty years later, he needed to renew the policy and wasn't sure how to go about it. He had taken Sundays for his own, catching up with the news, watching a game or two, preparing his week's work. Betty had stopped going to services after they'd sold the house.

As he went up the church steps, he murmured, "Hi! I'm Harold Fryer." There was no response. He didn't really expect God to lean down and say, *Well am I ever glad to see you, Hank,* or even, *Where the hell've you been?* but he would have liked to feel a touch on his shoulder, a reassuring puff of holy breath on his cheek, a sudden warm glow as he reached the top step. And there was nothing! At least the All-Seeing hadn't given him a shove and pushed him down the steps and into the street.

He was here because premiums must be paid in advance. Right! A rule. A fact of accident and life. A matter of common sense. There is no such thing as insurance after the event. Fires and accidents can't or shouldn't be foreseen. *Mine is not a morbid occupation,* he said to those who asked. It's life-enhancing work. It gives comfort and provides a cushion, emotional ease to men and women whose lives are often stressed enough without them having to worry about fire and flood.

All his working life, not counting the stretch at Happy Hamburger and two summers resurfacing roads, he had gone into rooms with his hand outstretched saying, *Hi, I'm Harold Fryer and I'm with Midway Insurance.*

"Tell people your name, what you do, make yourself clear to them right off the bat. Start out straight," his first manager, old Crowley, had said as if after that he could make any crooked turns he liked.

He'd left Betty at home getting ready for their trip, listening to the radio, to a memorial concert for a singer he'd never liked. Once when their talk had briefly gone beyond the day-to-day, Betty had told him she knew a woman like Marlene Dietrich would have understood her. And he, laughing, had replied that all the star understood was sex and money. Looking back now he could see that was the wrong response. She had cried then. But the tears on her cheeks this morning were as much for her dad killed in the war as for the singer or for any of the usual reasons. And if she won-

dered what had provoked him to go to morning service all of a sudden, she was too caught up in the
music to ask.

Harold stepped inside the church nodding to the
ones he knew. A few of his customers were there taking out a different kind of policy on life, insuring themselves for afterwards if there was an afterwards, though
in this place he knew he had to suppress all doubt.
Some of them responded to his nod with the specially
bright smiles of the saved, pleased to welcome him, the
sinner, to the lowest rung of the ladder.

I took the straight option, he informed God as music engulfed the church and a smattering of feet on tile
told him the service was about to begin. Under the
music he heard his own thought repeated over and
over: *I loved her as she set out on the water.*

He had expected the church to feel more homelike.
The church of his boyhood had been as much bake-
shop as House of God with the women all the time
having sales and brewing up potluck suppers and
strawberry teas. His dad had quit going because he said
that whatever the time of year the damn church
smelled like Thanksgiving. His mother had replied it
was no call to turn heathen, but his dad said he wanted
to spend his one day off weeding the garden and if
heaven was going to reek of turkey then he'd prefer to
spend eternity elsewhere, thank you very much.

There was a shuffling all around, and he knelt in his
pew and said without speaking, *Hi, I'm Harold Fryer.
Remember me? I know it's been a while.*

Voices in unison murmured responses he had
long forgotten and covered the words that crowded
into his head.

It's a small private lake, Betty. On Monday evening, others will be making their way back to the city. We'll have privacy.

Well I'd like quiet.

Meet me outside the church in an hour.

This church smelled of cheap floor polish. It was stark, modern. Its pillars were wooden masts, its walls were blocks, its windows coloured glass; no patterns, no stories told in large mosaic tiles. Just a few wooden boards on the walls dedicated to special people. To Glenda Warbin for courageous service. To certain soldiers killed young. To benefactors.

Standing up to sing, the people began to work their way into "The Lord's my shepherd." He remembered the words but they were singing them to a different tune. He tried to follow with "I shall not want. He leadeth me. He leadeth me beside," but they got ahead and lost him. And he could still hear in his head the words of the pagan song that had followed him from the house that morning: *Who'd want to cry when he says goodbye to a sweetheart. . .*

It was cold, this church, like the one they were married in. He'd hardly noticed the building that day, full as it was with lace and hats and relatives. There had been an altar and a tapestry behind it with woven figures of men fishing. He'd kept his eye on that and tried to remember his lines. IdoIdoIdoIdoIdon't. *Meet me at the church at noon, Betty.*

You've got a good one there, his dad said at the reception. But neither of them had noticed that under the wing of dark hair, the bride's mouth turned down and her eyes could darken in seconds like a storm getting up over a lake. And how suddenly she could become silent. Silent like water still after rain, like water closing over a head.

You need insurance, Mrs. Belchuk. Insurance helps you sleep easy at night, lets you know that whatever disaster happens, you're not going to be out on the street. Things happen when you least expect. Midway takes care of its customers. And I will take care of you.

Harold had never lived in dangerous countries or known how to starve or lie behind rocks and shoot at people who might have been his brothers or neighbours. He'd never even damaged the car and fire had not eaten up his belongings and left him homeless. Burglars stayed away from his house. So surely he was a good risk. *Just this one thing, Almighty Shepherd.*

The music stopped. All around him, people listened carefully to the words of the lesson as if He could really see the sparrow fall and the hungry man weep and the woman drown.

Harold recalled some tale from long ago about a woman drowning in her own tears, and in a way that's what Betty had done. When her face came to him in nightmares now, it was through streaks of water like a rainy day through glass.

A gathering of boys and girls, knowing sweet nothing, lifted their voices to holler *Alleluia*. And then sang words in such a high key that they hurt his ears.

Insure against flooding, Mrs. Belchuk. Rare in this area but not unknown. Call it water damage. I've seen a piano ruined, books destroyed, wallpaper down in shreds. The premiums are nothing compared to the peace of mind I am offering you.

The terms coming through to him in this place were

similar to his own, familiar, reassuring. Be not afraid, you are insured with the best. We stand by our policies. As long as you have paid in time.

On their wedding night Betty had said gleefully— there had been pleasure then—"What have you done, Harold Fryer?" When he had sold their house and bought their so-much-easier-to-care-for condo, she had said it again in a different way. And had begun to cry. And had not stopped since. *Three years of crying, Lord*, he said remembering the right title. *Lord, how she has cried.*

The clergyman in his modern brief pulpit leaned down and looked directly at Harold and said, "I have taken as my text, 'The foolish body hath said in his heart, there is no God.'"

He was going to talk about casting them into the fiery furnace. Harold could feel it coming on. He wished he had with him the old illustrated prayer book that had given him comfort in similar times long ago with its pictures of lambs and gentle women in blue and white. But being a modern man, this priest began to talk wilderness and left hell to the imagination. Hell was local. Hell was custom-made. Hell was another person.

Who'd want to cry when he says goodbye to one sweetheart, since another is waiting round the next corner.

He could see Betty now in the meeting with the lawyer when they were selling the house, and it had sprung out at him how she would always set up an alliance with the other one. He hated the way she did that when they were in an office or wherever. Almost right away. She would do it now if she were here in Church with him. She would be nodding at the Lord, saying little asides: *Well yes, poor Harry, always been colour blind, always had a problem, talks too much, doesn't know about values, supposed to be so smart. Take no notice of him, God!*

The preacher went on, "Nothing is hidden. God who is inside each of us, like a scanner, knows . . . "

By the lake, they would say, seeing him there, white, splashed, silent, *Give him hot strong coffee. Get him away. He shouldn't see this. It's terrible. Poor man. He's in shock. Keep him warm. Make him lie down. The police will want to talk to him.*

Hi, my name is Harold Fryer. My mother wanted me to be a doctor but I sell insurance. It is not such a life-threatening job. Your future is my future, Mrs. Belchuk.

We know this is a terrible blow, Mr. Fryer, but there are some questions.

"And like a scanner, reading not only the thoughts and plans but also the excuses, the reasons we give to ourselves when we are about . . ."

Why was your wife out in the boat alone?

Did you know she had set out?

The weather is sudden on this lake.

Hi my name is Harold Fryer.

Were you a devoted couple?

Did you know that your boat had a split seam?

Had you been heard to say you were going to caulk it next time at the lake?

You didn't prevent her from going?

My name is Harold Fryer.

You didn't prevent her from going!

She was a wilful woman.

Water had become the centre of their lives. She

talked and cried. He boiled water for tea. *Drink this, dear. I'd be better if I could, Harold. A warm bath is soothing. Why can't we afford a Jacuzzi? Or go to the sea? A week by the lake. We can get a cottage. Take the canoe. I want to stay at a lodge. Not be cooking and cleaning. What kind of a break is that for me? And you're too old for a canoe, Harold. But Fred's cottage has all mod cons, honey.*

The canoe was tied to the top of the car all ready for the journey. That evening they would settle into the cabin. For all her sorrow she packed food that was good, fruit, cheese, bread, soft drinks.

Neither of us drinks alcohol, Lord/sergeant.

First it was because we couldn't afford it. Then we saw what it did to our friends.

She takes the canoe out in the sober morning.

Go on Betty, go on. You used to be a whizz at it.

She smiles and is cheered by the sight of rocks and pines.

I could have been happy here.

Take the paddle. Go on. I'll watch.

Won't you come with me?

We can't change our lives now, honey.

He had customers who liked him, who depended on him. He had Francie and didn't want to lose her. Francie had laughter where Betty had tears. Francie knew delight. And Francie needed his love. He needed hers.

Was your wife well insured?

Naturally.

For a large sum?

Fifty thousand dollars is not more than you might win in a lottery any weekend, eh Lord?

But there had to be an accounting. No one knew more about audits and bottom lines than he did. Payments came due and the balance sheet had to be kept straight. He'd taken out insurance on his life at a good price years ago. Prudently. Prudently. Betty, in the event of his death, provided for. And now here he was taking out an all-inclusive for his soul.

He saw her getting up pleased next morning, smiling, commenting on the trees, the shimmer on the lake, the cool clean night air. She would go out alone but was a little scared, a little held-back. It was, for her, a definite act, something she had to do to prove that there would be fewer tears in future. He would look at her lovingly, loving her less as her toes touched the water and she drew her foot back in a silly shrieking way. She wasn't young, after all.

Take the canoe, sweetheart. Go on. Go on.

The guy up front there, wrapped in white, had spent his life going up to people saying, Hi, I'm Michael, your friendly priest, my insurance policies cost nothing, only every Sunday of your life and some weekdays and a voluntary contribution. And in return you get a time-share in paradise. Cheap at twice the price. But what did he know!

His voice was drawing them to a close. *Now let thy servants depart.* Organ notes poured out and rose higher and filled up the space, driving the congregation away, making them hurry to the door.

God knows he knows the boat is a touch weak but no one is asking her to stand up out there and tip the boat over. He is only waving. She has no need to wave back.

The breeze came up from nowhere, sergeant.

As he walked out of the church, he said to the waiting priest, "Hi! My name is Harold Fryer."

And the priest, young in his black and white outfit, aware of evil but knowing nothing of its reality, replied, "I know."

Harold, startled, stepped back almost falling down the stone steps. The clergyman reached out to hold his arm. Smiled at him, became his saviour. And Harold knew. He saw now, as he stood there, all of it, the plan, the intervention from above. In detective stories they said to watch for that moment when the ordinary man does something out of character. *You went to church Harry Fryer,* a thousand accusing voices shouted at him, screeching like crows. *For the first time in twenty years!*

"You sold me my first policy," the priest said.

"Ah. Yes," Harry replied but it was too late.

Fear had struck at his soul like a cold steel knife. In that moment he knew that he was known. All his thoughts, the half-formed plans, were visible. Bloody murder was written on his brow for all to see.

Francie Francie Francie Francie, he cried out silently, bitterly, feeling tears on his own face as he ran down the steps.

He called out, "I was only going to tell my wife the truth." And was unheard against the noise of traffic.

In the parking lot by the hatchback, there was Betty, make-up covering the sad skin under her eyes, trying to smile as she secured the rope that held the canoe on top of the car. She was wearing her blue and grey leisure outfit, waiting for him to drive her to the vacation that was to solve all their problems. His and hers. He held the door open for her and walked round and got into the car beside her.

"I think it's going to be a dry week," she said.

"Let's hope so, honey," Harold replied as he turned the car towards the North. "Let's hope so."

THE
YELLOW
CANOE

"Yellow," Peter said.

Myra let him get away with his 'yellow' because it was the first positive thing he'd said in weeks and she was downright tired of snipping the ends off string beans. Anything to get him out of his garden. He'd been working out there with a sullen kind of energy ever since he'd let slip he was afraid of dying.

"Isn't everybody," she'd said, hurrying out of the door with her Stop sign and her orange vest. She regretted later not paying attention to him, not saying to him that when she thought about it, it gave her the creeping heebie-jeebies too. Death.

"Yellow," he said again.

The nearby lake had a coliform count well over the reasonable limit and no one was advised to trail a hand in the water let alone fall into it. It wasn't only a matter of the internal organs, but the skin could turn a peculiar shade if not actually break into a mottled rash. Peter, not caring about all that, thinking most likely of cleaner lakes a bit farther away, murmured something about the bark of the birch tree.

Out for their walk the Sunday before, they'd watched as a family of three piled into a canoe, loaded it with a cooler, and set off. They hadn't spoken, that family, mother, father, daughter, but had begun to paddle intently, each of them knowing exactly what to do, making a clear line across the lake towards the far shore. And Peter had stopped still in a kind of dream, muttering something about sunbeams on the water.

Myra had felt the magic of that silent moment also. So after breakfast she tidied up, put a touch of rose pink blush on her cheeks, a purple comb in her hair to hold it back, donned her blue jacket that was wearing a bit thin but still looked smart, and followed him out to the car.

"Yellow," he repeated.

When he'd returned to Canada in '48 and she'd followed on, she'd expected adventure and now it was quite overdue. It was a long time since they'd amazed each other or anyone else for that matter. Perhaps it was time. Peter beside her was humming a tuneless tune, recalled from his two summers at camp. She was remembering the day by the lake when she'd seen him kissing Amber Papadakis, her faithless childhood friend, and Amber had left without a word next day, lost again to her world of dimly lit theatres.

The Discover Your World store smelled like the inside of a tent on a hot day. There was everything: ropes, stoves, lamps, tents, boats, axes, hiking boots, mountain bikes, water bottles, backpacks, knives for skinning animals, inflatable rafts, hats that were rainproof and pans that fitted inside other pans. There were coolers, bikes that folded, and boots for climbing. The whole place shrieked of danger.

Peter and Myra stood silent before it all as if they were already started on their journey, hung about with equipment, perched on a Himalayan slope, or moon-walking deep below the ocean taking pictures of one another swimming with dolphins.

The salesman, more like salesboy, came up to them and said, "Can I help you?"

"A canoe," Peter replied, continuing decisive. "We want to buy a canoe."

The slim boats were strung up on the wall like or-naments. Beautiful in their shape. Blue, yellow, brown. Not one of them was made of the bark of the birch tree.

The boy in his jeans and T-shirt said, "The four-teen-foot one weighs about fifty-five kilos. Comes in at around nine hundred dollars. We might include the paddles. Even throw in the cover. It's getting kind of late in the season."

A hundred odd pounds! Myra was finding it difficult these days to lift five pounds, let alone eleven times that. And as for Peter, he puffed and wheezed for min-utes after he carried the groceries into the kitchen. But he was standing there staring at the yellow canoe on the wall as if he were capable of portaging it on his head round Niagara Falls.

She said, "We have to discuss this. Considering we have to get a roof-rack and life jackets and there's tax. We could be looking at more than a thousand dollars."

"Paddles," Peter said.

"I have a lightweight one," the boy said, not re-leasing them.

"We'll go away and talk it over."

"Costs a little more. Around twenty-three hundred dollars. Could throw in the life jackets."

Peter had his belligerent I'll-take-three look on his face, a look provoked lately by salesmen who patronised him, who knew he was living on a pension, who wanted to save him money. What the salesboy saw was an elderly man with wispy grey hair, blue slacks, a green cotton shirt and a jacket he'd bought for five dollars at Goodwill. He couldn't see the one-time Union official, spare-time soccer coach, erstwhile lover.

"We'll have lunch and come back," Myra said.

Peter trailed out of the store behind her, followed her to the Vital Signs Cafe for lunch, not catching up, acting like a disappointed boy.

"We'd have to get used to it," he said. "That's all."

"It's more than that."

"My father. Those photos. Of him in a punt on the Thames."

"Your father in that picture was less than thirty and besides no one ever asked him to put the punt on the top of his motorbike or carry it round the locks."

Myra's own memory of boating was on the pond in the park, threepence an hour. An hour of bumping into other boats, trailing your hand in the mucky water, crossly returning when the man shouted your number. *Come in fourteen. Your time's up.* That was all long ago when life was still full of surprises and you could buy an hour of pleasure for the equivalent of half a cent in today's money. But that call, harsh and mean as if it was always only fifty-five minutes and never the full hour, had stayed in her head like an old echo. *Come in number fourteen.*

She watched the people drifting into the cafe. All

the different hairdos, pink, spiked, clothes all ragged and baggy. How was it possible to be outrageous any more? What could a person possibly do to make another person turn and stare these days? Only maybe walk in with his genitals hanging out, and today even that wouldn't make people take a second look.

In their decor, the management had tried for strange, but assorted dinosaurs and antique cookie boxes on a shelf above the juice machine didn't succeed.

The waiter put corn bread on the table in a basket and took their orders for one veggie sandwich and one soup of the day.

"If I could have lived at any time I chose," she said to Peter. "If I could have chosen my century, it would've been the last one. Imagine all the surprise of trains, electricity, telegraph."

"Every age has its surprises," Peter replied, not understanding.

"What lately has amazed you?" she asked.

There were crumbs round his mouth, and given half a chance he would list unfolding leaves, the sudden flight of birds, the rise and fall of tides. But she turned her head to look at the shiny coffee machine that whirred and groaned and churned out coffee not much better than instant.

She passed half the sandwich to him. He began on the soup and would leave half of it for her. He sipped and nodded. It was good soup.

The waiter came and stood by their table. His infinite hairy legs rose up into the shortest shorts and the little apron in front made him seem like an exploited waitress of earlier and perhaps present times. Myra wanted to reach out and put her hand on his thigh but held back.

"Is everything satisfactory?" he asked.

"No it isn't. There's nothing amazing here."

"We try," he said. "But there's no way we can keep up. We truly strive for surprise. We change the menu daily. We hire and fire staff like it's a revolving door. I took Phenomena as a major at university and look where it got me."

"My wife's been reading," Peter said trying to explain her away as he had done in the past but had not bothered to do lately. "I'll have your fruit pie with cream. If the cream's fresh."

"I'm always hoping for something new myself," the waiter said, waiting. "You've got to keep your eyes open."

"And I'll have an oatmeal square, please," Myra told him.

Peter said to her, "We'd use it on sunny mornings."

"Mornings!"

"There's a lot of good weather left. It's quiet after the kids go back."

And this year the kids were going back without her. She'd taken the job on as a kind of volunteer thing after the wool and fancy needlework store closed down due to lack of custom and left her free. She hadn't expected there to be an age limit on seeing kids across the road three times a day. She'd loved their cheerful morning faces, the bits of their lives they told her as they waited for her to give them the go-ahead. Her eyes weren't perfect but she could still see cars coming for cripe's sake. But in June the council had taken her reflector jacket and her Stop sign away and said, Thank you very much, goodbye. So she was free for the first time in the fall. Probably forever. Till her number was called.

"We'll go back and look," she said to Peter, to let him down gently.

Getting a canoe had been a moment's silly dream. A mad idea. Kim and her friend Sharon would laugh their heads off and tell their friends that the old folk had finally lost it. Imagine at their age!

He was thinking about his father in the punt. His mother lying back there with her hair in a long braid over her shoulder. *A girl light as a feather who brought the moonlight and the starlight.* They weren't married then, his parents. They were a couple ahead of their time. In that postwar madness, the twenties, they'd lived out a kind of homage paid to the lost ones, living two lives if they could, living on behalf of the dead. And then emigrating to the New World to give their boy a better life.

"We might be able to lift it."

"Our feet would get wet," she said.

"I don't mind that."

She wanted him to mind. She wanted him to wince when he put his feet in that chill water and feel the sharp pain in his calf muscles after. And the rest of the day and lie awake at night twisting and turning. She wanted him to cry out in agony as he had when she'd accidentally unwound his Marlene Dietrich cassette. The new ones, he'd said when she'd offered to replace it, had nothing like the same quality.

The salesboy was surprised to see them back. In his experience, customers who said they were going to talk it over didn't return. And these two old folks! Humour them. Maybe they had more money than they showed.

"We've come to try your canoe," Myra said. "If you could just get it down off the wall."

The boy and another young man reached for it with two sticks with hooks on the end, and lowered it to the ground. And there it stood, a streamlined shell of curved wood, painted, metal tips, waiting only for two adventurers.

Peter bent down at the bow. She took the stern. They each got a grip of it and tried to lift it. Six inches off the ground only and she felt the old sharp pain in her stomach and let go of it. He dropped his end and gasped.

The boy kindly said nothing for a moment.

Peter stood there looking around him at little things, at the floats stacked three deep, the waterwings, the frisbees.

"About all we could do in that is grow geraniums," Myra said. "Even if we could get it home."

"You can rent a canoe by the hour," the boy said. "Place by the lake. They'll put it in the water for you."

Peter was making paddling motions, muttering about birch bark again.

The boy, in his glance, sized them up not only as old but lost to reality and said, "You know. And get it out again."

Peter began to walk away, leaving her standing there.

"Wait a minute," Myra said, so loudly that other people turned to stare.

And then, because Peter's dreams had been stamped on too often, she said to the salesman, "Let's look at your lightweight one."

They had bits of money here and there. There was

nothing worth watching on TV these days anyway and the old set could last a while longer. They could save too on heat in winter.

The boy came towards them easily carrying another perfect canoe. He set it down at their feet.

"Oh," Peter said stroking the side of the lovely boat, "It's not yellow but it's pretty near the same colour as birch."

The young fellow helped them get the fine brown boat outside onto the brand new roof rack and put the life jackets in the trunk. The paddles were the best they had, he said, light and strong. He offered them respect and waved as they drove down the street.

When they got home, Peter got out and limped round to open the door at her side. As she stepped out of the car, he kissed her.

"Come on, Hiawatha," she said, "let's lift it down."

One afternoon before long, afternoon because neither of them was all that agile in the morning, they would launch their craft, get their feet wet, and paddle off across the water to see what was on the farther shore. Without fear. And even, Myra thought, as she found a place for the paddles under the stairs, if the sun was shining and they were feeling good, even with joy.

THE
HOBBY

Almeida knew that other women's husbands had inno-
cent hobbies. She had met men in bars and in theatres
and occasionally on horseback who talked of electric
trains, of rare stamps, or of birdsong. One day when
she was standing up to her hips in water, the man beside her asked if she would like to buy an entire box
full of matchbox covers. She loved him at once for his
ordinariness, but just then a fish tugged at his line and
pulled him farther out into the river.

It was not that Joe had maliciously chosen to fill the
house with imitations of her, it simply seemed beyond
his power to stop. The counsellor had said, "A retired
man needs a hobby," as if she, Almeida, was the villain
in this piece. For a while she had accepted that role.
She had swept and tidied where she could and set
meals down on stairs and in corners and tried to tell
him that her hair had never looked like that. And then,
when there seemed to be no way of getting his attention, she had decided to 'distance herself from the
problem.'

So he had his hobby, she had hers. She bought tickets. He bought wood. She bought maps. He bought new
chisels. She moved around the country and wrote postcards to him and to the children from far away. She
took photographs and stood up in small boats to see
better views and heard her own voice talking too loudly
to strangers. He stayed at home and carved her features out of maple and gave her the fifties hairdo of a
Dietrich, the proud look of a beautiful woman.

Last month, out there in the mountains, she had
begun to think that she was wasting too much time on
scenery. She had to stop reaching out to it and endow-
ing it with magic. She had allowed rocks and waterfalls
to offer her lifelines. She had lived by scenery, as
though it were her own soul but external. And now it
was time to walk backwards away from all that gran-
deur and become a person who asked the advice of
others.

The fact that Joe had been right about the West was
not in his favour. It only meant that he had been in that
place in his youth, without her, singing perhaps, enjoying himself, nice, his hands still. And that he had,
somewhere, underneath all those heads, some pictures
of his own.

"Be patient," the counsellor had said to her and had
gone on to explain the sudden-peace syndrome. Men
and women of Joe's age, brought up to fight, ready, even
eager to go over there and kill or be killed, had been
stopped by the surrender of the enemy. Peace had broken out and side-lined them. Allowances had to be
made. But that was nearly fifty years ago, she had replied,
and surely time had cured them of their belligerence.

She sat in the living room across from Jean and

dipped a hard oatmeal cookie into her tea. Bits were left floating in the cup. It was not attractive.

"You've been back two days," Jean said.

"Do I have to keep going away?"

"Have you confronted him?"

Confront, they said. *Be aggressive. Go to assert-iveness class. It's your house too.* She had heard those words often. She had heard irritation in the voices which spoke the words out loud. Seen anger on the faces of her daughters. But all of it was easy to say. When she heard them saying it, she felt homesick for canyons and crevasses and the very edge of the land.

So she said, "I've come back to tell him, to offer him love, to consider, I think, starting over."

Jean said, "He must notice when you're not there."

"Half the house is mine."

"But he takes up all of it. You should have half, Almeida. You paid for half."

That too was easy to say when halves were so hard to define. What if, in each room, she owned the upper half where the air was better? Maybe the rooms could be divided in a zigzag way allowing her certain unclut-tered parts. Or perhaps the outer shell of the house was all hers, the brick walls, the red-tiled roof, the chim-ney; and the inner space all his.

"Well I might move away for good."

"Some people wonder why you haven't. Why haven't you?"

Even the best of the mountains had given Almeida no answer to that. Last Wednesday, standing on the shore of the Pacific, she saw that she could go no fur-ther unless she seriously considered flight. And so she had returned home to confront, to be assertive, to make up her mind.

She gritted her teeth and moved on to the second reason for her visit. Jean had been friend and neighbour for years. But exasperation and age had come between them. And a certain amount of envy. After all, she could, she did, travel at certain times for weeks, cheaply and by bus, but still it was travel, it was getting away. Jean stayed at home and her home was at least three-quarters hers. Her thirty-year-old son stayed in his room much of the time. *Dwayne is designing a new boat*, was the fiction they all maintained.

Jean now sitting opposite her there, wearing a pair of neat blue slacks and a loose sea-green top, had become an older woman, a woman with dried skin and brown-spotted hands and an odour of stale perfume. *Always dab a little bit on here and there.* That Jean was her mirror image with different features, Almeida well knew. Your trouble, Almy, her mother had said, is you can see too much. And that, too, was true.

"Jean!" Well she had come out with the first part, the name. Her friend looked back at her slyly waiting for her to drop the other shoe.

"Jean. I want your advice. What would you do now, if you were married to Joe?"

"Do you mean you're going to hit him or something?"

"I've made some enquiries. Legal enquiries."

They could hear Joe's electric lathe through the wall. He was beginning something new. There he was next door, there he was, there he was sure to be, at eleven in the morning, chipping, splintering, working his way towards perfection.

When I've made one perfect one, I'll quit. Three

years ago he had promised that. And that was when the faces were still in the basement and the wood chips had to be carried out in sackfuls on Fridays only.

"I know you tried to persuade him to move to the country."

"The housing market's down now."

"They're going to want to know why you didn't leave?"

"I've been everywhere I can."

Now that Jean was more of a critical spectator, understanding could be expected on some days and not others. This was a day when her affection was shown in the tea and the brittle home-made cookie. And how could you tell a friend that she didn't put enough shortening in her recipe, that oats swelled as they cooked, they sucked in moisture?

"Here. I'm offering you a room."

Tears came to Almeida. Tears she hadn't been able to shed in Vancouver or Jasper or Rocky Mountain House now made it hard for her to see. This was sacrifice. In Jean's neat and flowery home there was room for her, there was a space at least five foot nine and forty inches at the widest point wide.

Almeida said, through her tears, "I'd like another of these delicious cookies, please." She had come to her friend for advice and had been given love. It was very hard to bear.

"Well I mean it."

She touched Jean's hand and returned to the house next door. Her suitcase, she always managed with only one, was still in the hall. And the sound of the lathe was a high-pitched deterrent to conversation. Nevertheless she had to speak.

In their house, the faces looked at her from every wall and from the floor. Some of them were tilted, others frowned, some were in profile, others full face. And they were her own eyes that looked at her but wooden, without irises, plain dead eyes like the eyes of ancient statues.

Joe sang as he worked. He was a happy ridiculous man. And that was why until now, until this moment when the chairs in the dining room were filled with replicas of her, when on every step there was a left head and right head, and the spare room was so full of heads the door would scarcely open, she had not driven him away. She had been the one to go, to pack up and say, "I'm going on a little trip, I'll be back soon." And she had left him there singing and chiselling and answering the phone.

"Some man called," he said, looking up now from the bench in the kitchen. "Some man called Eric phoned. Eric. I asked him to spell it."

"When did he call?"

"Last Thursday, I think?"

"Did he say what about?"

"About a fishing trip."

"The travel agent?"

"He said his name was Eric."

"You could've told me before."

Joe was wearing old grey slacks and a shirt that had once been blue and a rag round his neck. He wore gloves now to protect his hands and worked more slowly than he used to. As she came past him, he turned the block of wood he was working on away from her as if it were a private letter, something not to be seen.

"Any offers?"

"I think I got it right, Almy."

"Can I look?"

"Not yet. It's not quite finished."

He took off his apron and set it down on the floor with a jangle of metal. The pockets for his hammer and his chisel and screwdriver had been stitched by her years ago after she had read about the wonder of hobbies, their help in curing depression and overcoming the ennui of a nine-to five life, and their absolute necessity in retirement.

How pleased she had been to find him working there at his new bench in those first weeks when he was at home all day and she still had six months to put in at the store. And how pleased she had been to see how quickly his depression had lightened. He had taken to singing again, and once she had caught him leaping about the room in a dance of celebration.

Now he sat down on the edge of a chair that contained two heads and listened. He listened to her traveller's tales without hearing, his eyes fixed on her face. At last when she had come down from the mountains and back through the valley, he said, "It's nice to have you home."

"I've been back two days," she said. She had cleared a month's laundry away, swept two months' crumbs up off the kitchen floor, and appreciated the fact that there were no heads in the bathroom.

"Staying now?" he asked.

His own face was younger and brighter than it had been. He had shaved that day and his hair was combed. There was a look of triumph to him. There was wine in the fridge that had not been there when she left. She leaned across to him and smiled and said, "Perhaps."

By the river, by the mountains, she had sworn to give it another try. There had been love in this house once. Love had shrieked its existence from the walls and the ceiling. The girls had not been able to stand it and both had left as soon as they could to build lives with loves of their own. But there had been love here, in these very rooms. And she had returned to remind him of that.

Either the heads go or I do. That had been an old argument of long ago. After she retired, she had said that. And he had come towards her with his chisel and explained that this work gave his life true meaning.

Later she would negotiate for space of her own. She would insist on boundaries while at the same time letting him know that his carving was improving head by head. Way back there in the early years, they had laughed together. They might do that again. They might travel and climb the easier mountains side by side.

Before she went to bed, she got a turkey out of the freezer. A small one for a festive meal to which she could invite Jean and Dwayne, and she would make, among other things, her special salad.

He came to bed a little while after her and took her in his arms and said nothing for a long time. Then he made love to her in a ritual fashion as though one of the wooden heads had sprouted a wooden body. But that too could change.

Leaving him in their bed, snoring, his face to the wall, she crept downstairs to look at the new head. She had to put the light on and then stand and listen to make sure she was alone before she could reach out and turn it towards her. It was of darker wood than the others, and it felt sticky to touch, almost like skin. It was the head of a beautiful woman. He had given this one a lean nose, narrow cheeks, eyes with pupils, eyes that looked at her now, questioning her rights.

"Who are you?" she asked the head. After all it had ears. It had small ears, perfectly placed. Its mouth was uneven, the side of the lower lip had a slight cast to it as though it was drawn back, drawn in over the teeth. And there was an insolence, a kind of possession to this head, a feeling of power. Almeida set it down quickly. She knew exactly who it was.

She cleared a space on the floor so that she could lie down and calm herself. She breathed deeply and cast her mind around for pleasant memories. Times were when Joe had taken her and the girls to the park, when she had packed a picnic for them all and he had sung bright songs and played an imaginary guitar and all of them had joined in the chorus.

Her conscience was clear.

She had tried many times to stare him into reality.

She had only once stood over him with the chisel in her hand, only once been tempted to change that face of his while he slept.

She went upstairs and put a nightgown and a tooth-brush into her flight bag and a photograph of the two of them in the old days standing in front of a palm tree in California. And she went down those steps and picked up her travelling case and opened the door and walked out of the house, quietly, before it got light. She walked to the road and began to run, her wheeled case clattering along the sidewalk.

The sound of the wheels shattered the silence just

as that woman had shattered their marriage. The wooden head, the last one, was the image of the only woman Joe had ever loved. His unattainable love. The woman who had ruined everything. The woman he had been trying to hold close to him for all these years. She was the rival, not all the carving, not all the faces, not the new pieces of wood he brought so carefully into the house. He had got it right at last. He had clearly carved out the face of the woman she should hate but could not. Herself! Herself in those first years. Herself at twenty-five. Herself when young. His one true love.

SOMETIMES I LOOK AT YOUNGER MEN

"Sometimes I look at younger men," Almeida said.

And she did. She looked at their biceps and triceps and quads in the gym, and at their still unfrightened faces. She saw that some of them had very hairy legs and others were smooth. She looked at young men on the street in their well-fitting suits or tight jeans. And at their hands and eyes. She looked at dark-haired ones and fair ones and those going prematurely bald.

"Sometimes," she said to Jean, "they look back at me."

But only Ivar when he looked back had told Almeida, in his awkward way, what he saw: a young woman in an older body trying hard to get out. His comment reminded her of Joe and his attempts to immortalise her young self in wood. But she smiled and held in her stomach, handed Ivar the files he wanted.

Like her, he slotted his twice-weekly trips to the Fitness Centre in the lunch break. Sometimes they walked there together from the office and then he mentioned how much he wanted to get on in the new country and how he missed his friends in Norway.

Almeida had kept Ivar's first note to her and pushed it across the table to Jean. Jean spread out the crumpled paper and saw that Ivar had written with true Scandinavian terseness: Mrs. Kerwell, there is not clips for the papers.

He'd been told, Almeida explained, that, in North America at least, God was still in the details.

Almeida had never been one of those people who could ration herself to one telling phrase and let *Come up and see me sometime* or *My dear, I don't give a damn* express a volume of feeling and thought. She spoke. She let words flow and her listeners could pick out what they chose.

Over lunch, she had begun a perfectly good conversation about the weather and worked through international conflict, pay-equity for women, the value of rehydrating cream, and brought it round to her father's love of hunting and his cavalier driving habits.

"My mother could have written the original roadkill cookbook," she said to Jean who was sitting opposite eating spinach salad and listening to her in the way that old friends do. Tolerating the repetition, waiting patiently to hear something new.

"My father could drive quite well when he wanted," Almeida said.

He'd driven her down the highway to her wedding thirty-six years ago without hitting a thing. But she had the impression that the wildlife on that day, hearing the sound of his engine, had backed into the forest out of the way.

"You know, like a movie rewound."

Jean nodded. And Almeida continued. Joe himself was a young man then, a boy of thirty with a fine round behind, firm pectorals, and thick brown hair that caught the light. Almeida stopped talking for a moment and considered this picture. Then she moved on.

The romance with Ivar, if she dared to call it that since no mention had been made of love or sex by either of them, had begun on a Thursday or maybe it was a Wednesday. At any rate, the sun was shining through the windows of Combined Charities Inc.; beams full of dust particles hit the papers and files. Both of them had reached for the same application. Their hands had touched.

When Jean suggested that she was responding to a deep and fleeting need, Almeida said, "Garbage!" Her life at the moment was full and pleasing. I mean you could have said that two years ago. Just after she'd walked out of her marriage. Those were bleak months and dry days. When she'd left Joe and his chisels and wooden heads, life hadn't exactly opened up like a fast river leading to the Sea of Opportunity. Some people said without putting it into those exact words, Well at fifty-six what do you expect! As if a flair for résumé writing and owning two decent outfits was not enough.

"As you know," Almeida told her friend, "I walked into that job at CCI as if I was the only applicant."

And there in the next office was Ivar, struggling with the language, reading every journal he could get his hands on, running around looking for help and advice, listening and then repeating phrases like a mynah bird.

The following week, she showed Jean his second, more intimate note. "Almeida," it read, "there are still not enough clips for the papers."

"What's with all the paper clips?" Jean asked.

"We have to gather material on would-be recipients and references and all kind of letters and background."

"Computers?"

"Back-up. Hard copy. Loss of power. All kinds of reasons. The original documents have to be saved."

"And you and Ivar work at the same desk?"

"He likes to talk to me."

Almeida turned away from the sceptical look on her friend's face.

"Paper clips were invented in Norway," she said. "By a Norwegian."

No one round the office mentioned the fact that Ivar was young enough to want children. No one mentioned that he was married because no one knew whether he was or not. They took it for granted that somewhere near Oslo a tall blonde on skis was standing in the snow calling out his name in vain.

What Almeida didn't say to Jean, given Jean's attitude which could well be based on jealousy, was that Ivar had looked back at her at the very moment when she had begun to wonder if her gestures were ridiculous and if her phrases were outdated. She had even begun to wonder if she looked like a man wearing women's clothes. Her face had taken on sharper lines the past few years; hairs sprouted one by one on her chin. Not that, she would have said to Jean if she'd been talking aloud, she had anything against transvestites. She just didn't want to appear to be one at that particular time.

Only that morning, Ivar had come into her office wearing running shorts and a sleeveless shirt and found her sitting at her desk staring into a mirror and not liking what she saw. He had taken her hand and kissed it in a way she associated more with French people than those from the chilly North.

She knew it meant nothing, but when he suggested that they have lunch together, it took all her self-control not to leap over her desk and hug him.

It wasn't what you'd call a date, sitting next to Ivar in the cafeteria. She talked to him and when she paused for breath, he talked to her. He was laughing because he'd read in *Time* that the Chinese had a learned committee for "The Investigation of Rare and Strange Creatures." Almeida wasn't sure if he considered her to be either or both or if he did, whether it was a compliment.

Later he made the remark about a sculptor and his block of marble and the figure trapped within it. But Almeida had heard that one before and couldn't help thinking that Ivar perhaps knew more about the language than he let on.

Almeida told Jean about her second lunch with Ivar, or was it the third, at least it was a Tuesday. It had to be Tuesday because it was the step class.

"We were eating tofu salad," she said, "in the cafe at the fitness place because they serve healthy food and we never have more than twenty minutes to spare. And Ivar told me that the Romans invented bingo."

"Fascinating," Jean said. And did not say, although Almeida could see she was thinking it, *you'd have been better off to stay with Joe.*

Almeida could still hear the sinister sound of wheels, little tinny wheels, following her along the sidewalk early in the morning, the day she walked away from her marriage dragging her suitcase.

Her children, forgetting the songs she had sung to them, the soup she had fed to them, the tears she had wept for them, remained distant. They had taken their father's side. Had she not told him to get a hobby? He had only done what she said! For that she had left him! And now, there she was cavorting, Geraldine said in reproach, with someone a third her age.

"Imagine," Almeida said to Jean. "Cavorting! Me. And he's not a third my age. That would make him nineteen."

"And a half," Jean said.

"And what does age matter? I can't help saying it, Jean. I know it's being said all the time. But age is only a number."

At work, Almeida listened to Ivar talk about Ibsen and the cold strong land he had left. She read *The Doll's House* and could see no happy future for that family. Those children would be scarred for life, she said to Jean but not to Ivar.

When Jean phoned, Almeida's fingers made sticky marks on the receiver. Her herring salad was still not turning out like the picture in *Norwegian Cookery for Beginners*. The kitchen was beginning to smell like a fish factory.

The next week, Jean had some talking to do herself. It was Almeida's turn to listen. Jean told Almeida that something about Ivar had reached Joe's ears through all the noise he made with his hammer and lathe. He had taken a meat cleaver and cut her head in half. Jean and Dwayne had listened in horror to these deliberate thuds on the other side of the wall. Chop. Chop. Chop. Joe had gone round the house and cut in half all the wooden images he had made of Almeida since he took up carving. He had made her into a left and a right side.

Almeida, her spoon dipping into her broccoli soup, felt like a split personality. She drew a line down the centre of her face with her finger and wondered how different the two sides of her head were. When he cut her sculpted head in two had he realised at last that she was no longer that young version of herself that he had loved? Could he come to love her as she was now, older, with some lines on her face, with scads of experience and two thirds of life behind her? Was he finally aware that she was no longer the twenty-two-year-old he couldn't bear to lose?

Jean was staring at her across the table but Almeida wasn't about to cave in.

"Good for him," she said.

"You're a hard woman," Jean replied.

Almeida put on a short blue dress with a tight skirt to meet Ivar for dinner. The rehydrating cream had softened her skin as advertised and the touch of lipstick gave her the look of an older aunt, not a long-married person with children but someone who has remained single and is gladly waving to the world from a good perch on the carousel of life.

At dinner, Ivar told her that more women than ever were marrying younger men. In Italy alone, he said, twenty percent of women married men eight to forty years younger than themselves. He had been given a copy of *Reader's Digest*.

Almeida invited Ivar to her apartment to look at her photographs of the fiords and glaciers in British Columbia that might remind him of his home. She waited, when she stopped talking, for him to lean across the table and ask her if she thought a romance with Andra in Personnel would be all right for him. But Ivar said no such thing. She waited for him to ask whether or not he should be more aggressive at the office. But he didn't say that either. She waited for him to hold her hand and tell her he was looking for a mother.

But Ivar told her that a thousand different kinds of birds inhabited the Galapagos Islands.

Attaching loops to the back, Joe was selling her profile for people to hang on their walls. So his hobby had after all become a profitable post-retirement occupation. Almeida called up her daughters to say to them in a pleasant way, I-told-you-so. But they were still uptight about her leaving their father and now betraying him with a young blond Viking. She heard envy in their voices and offered to baby-sit.

A dream more cheerful than a Bergman movie that had to do with warm dressing gowns and small cups of first-rate coffee began to invade her nights.

On the third Friday in March, a cold day, one of those winter-will-never-end days in Toronto, Almeida met Jean at the Blue Bear Bistro.

She said hello and ordered a bagel with cream cheese and smoked salmon and the purée of vegetable soup to start.

After several minutes, Jean said, "You're not saying anything, Almeida."

Almeida answered, "There's nothing to say."

Ivar had gone. No word of farewell. No phone call. Nothing except the empty space his 180 pounds of tall blond youth had occupied at the office.

Jean didn't respond but reproach stood between them like an indigestible plate of nachos with cheese and sour cream.

"I have been foolish," Almeida said when they met the next week, sliding gingerly into the booth. In response to Jean's look, she said, "The rowing machine! I don't usually use it but it was there. And I thought, why not."

Ivar had been using her to learn the language, to try out his unusual phrases, and had gone to a better life in Ottawa. Listening to her flow of talk was like an ESL course on disk, Andra had told her. Almeida stopped looking for letters or waiting for the phone to ring. Stopped wondering how she might justify marriage to a twenty-nine-year-old to her daughters.

She didn't mention Ivar's postcard to Jean the following week, but the message looped through her mind like the words of an old commercial: "Almeida, thank you for learning me so much of English. Your many words has helped desirably. Kind greetings, Ivar."

Jean knew better than to ask questions. She talked instead about Dwayne's new job and how, finally, he might be moving out to a place of his own.

Then she asked gently, "Will you go back to Joe?"

"Can he glue my head back together?"

"What's that supposed to mean?"

"It's not really me. I realised that. He was dreaming about all those glamorous women in movies in the forties and fifties. Merle Oberon, Rosalind Russell, Dietrich. The hair was a dead give-away. It wasn't me. It was who he wished I was."

"He's destroyed them now, Almeida."

"Do you know what I dreamt last night? I don't always dream, but last night I dreamt I was climbing up the side of an iceberg. It wasn't easy."

Almeida felt tears coming but held on and stopped them in their tracks. She understood now that she was guilty of exactly what she had blamed Joe for: not being able to let go of that youthful image and accept the older person.

"All the same," she said to her friend, "I will go on looking at younger men."

And she would, not because she expected to sweep one of them off his feet and into her bed, but simply because it gave her a great deal of pleasure.

BECOMING CHINESE

Almeida woke up that Monday morning wishing she were Chinese. She wanted to be small, delicate, and have thick, shiny black hair. She wanted to have come from Sichuan province and speak a difficult language and believe that she could have another chance at life. She wanted to be the best student in her calligraphy class.

It wasn't a dream that made her wish for oriental features but Jean's comment the day before about the passengers on the Dundas streetcar. "Have you noticed," Jean had said, "how exotic-looking, how lovely, all the people are except for us. Some of them are brown, some are a delicate taupe. Our skin is the colour of worms, our hair looks as though it's been in the dryer and . . ."

And!

"'And there is no health in us,'" Almeida had responded remembering an old prayer she'd recited often in church as a child, wondering all the while why this had to be said when most of the congregation were clearly as fit as fleas.

She stared into the bathroom mirror, hesitating to put on either the light or her glasses. They had set the clocks back. Daylight was increasing. Spring would very soon show up all her wrinkles and the mark on her cheek that she feared was cancer but was afraid to ask the doctor about. Her hair looked like a bad wig sprouting out in all directions, undecided whether to be grey or brown.

She put on her navy two-piece and decided to be late for work. They were still, behind her back, sniggering about Ivar. Only Andra in Personnel, who after all had been trained to deal with people, had complimented Almeida on the way she'd helped him with his English. "He left here much more fluent than he arrived," she'd said last week. "Thanks to you, Almeida." If there was sarcasm in her tone, Almeida chose to ignore it.

She had only ten more working days to go anyway. Even Combined Charities was down-sizing. And without putting it into so many words, Andra had suggested that now she was over sixty, it was time for Almeida to take up a more leisurely life. To get involved in nice pursuits like bridge and writing the family history. She should take satisfaction in performing charitable deeds for nothing.

"Leisure," Almeida said to Jean next day, "is a frightening word. It means time out. It means not having enough money to travel, sliding down the slope to darkness. Leisure is having time to tell the children whether I want to be cremated or buried. For working on the will. My grandmother knew all about leisure. She stitched forty-three Christmas tree quilts in her last ten years, and when she died she was knitting a toilet roll cover. I could easily sink into despair."

She saw Jean's look and moved on to a better topic. Jean had been at leisure for several years, and looking after her useless and almost middle-aged son couldn't have been as fulfilling as she liked to make out. Her friends referred to her behind her back as a martyr and sometimes as stupid for not having kicked the vegetable out into the street years ago.

To make up for her lack of tact, Almeida asked after Dwayne and let Jean tell her of his latest attempt to find work.

Walking up Spadina afterwards, Almeida began to think more about the Chinese approach to life and death. Why was it possible to consider a heaven and a hell and not, as millions of the earth's inhabitants do, the idea of a future life in a new role?

This thought was not flippant. It wasn't, *In my next life I'll be a thin blonde,* but rather, *I'll be a Chinese woman and leave my peasant roots and become a leader. An organiser of the downtrodden.* Or, *I will take the totally spiritual path and learn to exist without material goods.*

She skipped her next lunch date with Jean and went to the library. There was a great deal to know. At the farewell-and-thank-you party in the office, her head was so full of new thoughts that she scarcely noticed how celebratory the event was. They were happy to be able to fill her space with someone they thought was more efficient; she was happy to be free. Andra told her to make sure she had three meals a day and kept up her exercise regime. She gave her a pamphlet containing this and other good advice. Almeida threw it into the trash can on the way home.

Jean called her to say that if she needed company

now in this traumatic time, she would come and spend the day. Almeida said she wanted to go through the separation process alone. Jean mentioned Joe. Almeida said there was someone at the door and hung up.

The Chinese calligraphy instructor growled at the thinness of her down strokes. Wen Lo, she sensed, was not a happy man. Teaching these worm-coloured people fragments of his culture was perhaps not his idea of a life, and she wondered what he might have previously been. And did he look forward to a reincarnation in which he would be a mountaineer, a cowboy, a true artist? That philosophy gave a person immense scope, but she was not foolish enough to think she would have a choice in the matter. Like much else in life it was most likely a lottery. Worse still, it might be that one became in the next life what one deserved according to one's behaviour in this.

The teacher shooed them out of the room early. He looked tired and coughed frequently. Perhaps he hated them all for trying to attach themselves to a civilisation going back five thousand years of which they understood nothing but what they could see with their misshapen eyes.

She stopped in the Hunan Garden for green tea and almond cookies.

And there, peering into the window, was Joe.

Don't run away, was a precept she had been taught early on by a father who had faced down a moose bare-handed, so he said. And who had caught many a deer in his headlights and not allowed their pleading eyes to stop him in his tracks.

"Joe," she said.

"Come back to me," he pleaded fish-like through the glass with the streetcar rattling along Dundas Street behind him.

"Drop dead," she replied.

In the park behind the Gallery most mornings, old people were stretching out their arms and legs in a pantomime of slow aggression. She often stopped to watch. She liked the look of it. It would help keep her concentration and prevent her joints from seizing up.

When she finally got to the Tai Chi class, she was three weeks late and the instructor, a beautiful dark-haired woman in a white robe, waved her to a place and watched as she copied the moves of the person beside her. Almeida realised she had a long way to go before she could *grasp the bird's tail* in a truly Chinese way.

She mentioned something of her new life to Jean and Jean said, "Fortune cookies aren't mottoes to live by. They're the joke of a moment."

Dwayne had left, finally, just after his thirty-fourth birthday. Jean's very late empty nest syndrome was making her sharp, almost bitter. Her oatmeal cookies had become even harder. Her usual sympathy was lacking. She told Almeida she needed her head read.

In the classroom, Almeida found the overlaid glyphs very difficult to imitate. She wanted to work on the *Ling chih*, the Plant of Immortality, but Wen Lo set her on to the much simpler *Grain Measure*. With no idea of what she was putting on the paper, she feared that she was being crude. Wen Lo looked at her work and sighed his patient sigh.

As if he spent his life walking up and down Dundas Street in hopes of seeing her, Joe appeared at the teashop window again. It was raining a heavy April rain. She asked for another cup and beckoned him inside.

Joe said, "I've sold my chisels, I can get a new mortgage on the house, cut into my RRSP. Look."

He pushed a travel agent's brochure across the table. "Shanghai," he said.

"'It took more than one man to change my name to Shanghai Lily,'" Almeida quoted before she could stop herself. Decades ago they had fallen into the habit of trading lines from the movies for fun. James Cagney was Joe's specialty. The sexy superstars were hers. But that was when they were young. He was serious now.

"Beijing," he went on, "Xi'an. Yunan. The Yangtse River. Inner Mongolia. Sixty-three days. Fully escorted."

Green rivers and mountains and a sea of people looped through Almeida's mind. She sat back astonished not only at the itinerary but at the price.

Finally she pushed the shiny booklet back across the table. "Might as well be Mars," she told him.

She looked at his face and saw that she had been unkind. She tasted the tea and wished it was Orange Pekoe. Too much Tai Chi, too much awareness that she would never be able to make all the symbols of the mandarin lexicon were making her mean. The trapdoor finally opened and let into her consciousness the fact that she had been put out to grass like an old horse. Joe knew this. He knew how she had loved to travel.

He saw that she was looking into a long vacant space, just as he had done. He had filled his time with carving heads. Now to help her, he was offering a whole sub-continent.

"It's a lovely idea," she said. "Thank you, Joe."

"If you're learning to be Chinese," he said. "You might as well see where they live."

"How long could you afford to live if you spent all that money?"

He hesitated a moment before holding up his right hand with the fingers spread out.

She shook her head. It was just like him to go bar-relling on without any sense of proportion. Not for him the idea of making one or two or even three carvings of her head. He had made dozens. Filled the house. Till she'd had to leave, overwhelmed by images of herself.

"We could both go entirely broke," she said.

She pictured them landing on Geraldine's doorstep in a few years' time. All their household goods dumped on the sidewalk by a mover they hadn't been able to pay.

We're here, sweetheart, they would say in chorus in their old croaky voices.

The look on Geraldine's face in that scene wasn't hard to imagine. She loved her parents but couldn't stand them for more than one day, two at a stretch. Having discussed this with other parents, Almeida had come to see that a day was quite a long time and that she and Joe must after all have done something right.

"Entirely broke," she repeated.

Joe put the brochure back in his pocket and sipped the tea, pulling a face.

"We'd take our own teabags," he said.

*

"I was on the streetcar," Jean said, "and I saw you walking along with your nose in the air. What were you doing?"

"Inhaling," Almeida answered.

"I usually breathe through my mouth when I walk along past all that cabbage."

"Smells are as much a part of a culture as its music."

"Ah," Jean said.

"Guen chu chiu," Almeida replied.

"Why can't you learn French like everyone else?"

"Chinese music is exacting."

She had spent the evening before playing her new cassette of Chinese opera, trying to get used to the sounds. Even Wagner seemed more listener-friendly. Even hip-hop. It would take time and devotion.

"You'd be better off going back to Joe."

"If you're so keen, why don't you move in with him?"

Almeida saw at once that she had been mean again and said she was sorry.

"I've just finally got the house to myself," Jean said.

"Well you know what it's like then."

Joe met her at the teashop again with a different and much cheaper plan. Three days in Beijing, two days in Xi'an, a tour of Shanghai, a stopover in Korea and back home by the following Friday.

"And when we get back."

She knew he was about to suggest that she sublet her apartment, better still give it up, better even yet, move back to the house with him. She knew collusion when she fell over it. Jean and Joe. She could just see them wondering together what poor Almeida would do now with all her free time.

She looked at her ex-husband. A lonely man. Was it possible that if there was another life beyond this, they would return to earth as a pair of oxen harnessed together under a wooden yoke, ploughing fields in a remote Chinese province till they dropped? She said no to him as gently as she could.

Wen Lo invited her to his home. She was proud and pleased that of the fourteen students in his class, she was the chosen one. She looked around his living room. So quiet. So neat. Nothing unnecessary. And on the wall, two paintings. One of a bare tree against a pink background, lacy and delicate. She was drawn to the other, larger picture. The buildings, red with black roofs, were tilted this way and that as if they were made of flexible material. Tall buildings built of brick and stone but distorted, not made to last, shaken perhaps by an earthquake, pagoda-like shapes seen through a thin film of soft white petals.

"Beijing?" she asked.

"Ottawa in winter," Wen Lo answered as if it should be obvious.

She sat down opposite him and drank the tea he gave her. Took the soft cookies and ate them as if they might help her to be a better student. He talked to her about his home in China and suggested she give up calligraphy and take painting lessons. There were moments of silence. Someone was moving around in another room. She felt suspended in time. When she left, Wen Lo gave her a coloured fan.

She called Joe when she got home and met him next day at Second Cup on Bloor Street.

"I'll come to Shanghai," she said. "I'd like to see the Great Wall and the terra cotta army if we can afford it. I'll pay my way."

He looked at her. She looked at him, the aging image of the boy. Hair almost gone, a grey fringe round the back of his head, his complexion still clear, his eyes always with that enquiring sharpness in them.

He said quickly as if she might instantly change her mind, "You'd better get some shots and insurance and make sure your passport's up-to-date."

"What will the weather be like?"

"The annual average summer temperature in China is twenty degrees Celsius. And by the way, Almeida, maybe when we get back—"

"Ta ma da," she said. And without understanding a syllable of the language he knew when not to push his luck.

He was not stupid. There was more to being Joe than a bunch of chisels and filling in the time with patient reproduction and the air with sawdust.

"There is more to being me," she said to him, "than worm-pink skin and fried hair.'

"Your hair's fine," he said. "There's nothing wrong with your hair. It was pretty hard though to do in wood. It flew off in chips. Your hair, when it was long—" He stopped himself in mid-memory and began to drink his coffee.

"I'll bring a silk shirt back for each of the girls," she said, making lists in her mind.

"What made you change your mind?" Joe asked.

"Ottawa."

"The government!"

"There's more to being Chinese than making a few brushstrokes," Almeida replied.

She decided to walk home. Along Dundas. Through Chinatown. It was going to be a long march towards reality.

A
FAIRLY
FATAL
WOMAN

Once upon a time Jeanne had chosen the serious life. Made her decision. Save the world. Others before self. Feed the starving. Bring peace to the battle-weary. Order to chaos. Cry out against romantic postwar movies. Take the difficult route. But that had been decades ago. How very quickly she had been sidetracked! And now she was stuck like a train on a single line. There was nothing, it seemed, to be done but continue. No one could switch the track over and divert her to another route. No one. She looked round the room. Certainly none of these.

"More hot water, please," Jeanne called loudly to Pierre.

She had been intimate with this room now for thirty years though nothing that Robert had promised in the beginning had even hinted that she would spend long afternoons here, at ease in her admirable jacket. Over time, though she could only hear random words, she had come to know exactly what the people at the other tables were saying.

See the woman over there?

The red-haired one in the corner?

Who would dye their hair that terrible colour?

Grey hair goes like that when you put too much chemical on it.

But look at that jacket.

The jacket was blue shaded to red through purples and mauves. The sleeves were wide and gathered together at the wrist into black cuffs. A black band round the neck was held together by her gold initial. The wool was so fine that it shone like silk. She had bought it four years ago when Robert was about to leave. The very richness of it had consoled her in the moment for much of her lost life. And now she wore it in mourning for his lost life as well as hers.

The waiter approaching, the silver jug shaky in his hand, was older than she was. They were intimates. Their conversation had never risen above, *Cold day, Madame, Warm in here, Pierre. More tea, More water, Another of those delicious scones,* but they knew each other. She knew that he moved more slowly now. He knew that the lines on her face had been well-earned. They were both aware that they had been preserved here at the right temperature and would last forever like exhibits in a museum.

Years ago she had brought Georges here to the Ritz to tea. Or was he called Gilles, that one? She should remember *his* name for goodness sake! Fifteen years ago. No, more like eighteen years. She had been forty and he was a man of outstanding sexual stamina. Geoffrey? A very physical man not ashamed to cry out. It could have become a lasting relationship. But after the incident he, the nameless one, (*his* amnesia was brief), phoned her less and less often and then became silent.

Lovers holding hands came and sat down intently at the next table. He was wearing a worn leather jacket and she was in black, a large cheap scarf of many colours swirled around her shoulders. What was this place to them? Why had they come here? A celebration? An act of persuasion?

"I'm pleased that you remember-r-red," the young man said, switching languages. And the girl held her hair bunched up on the top of her head with one hand and shifted on her chair.

Jeanne poured herself a cup of tea watching the brown liquid flow in a smooth stream. In spite of all, *her* hand was still steady.

It's only the lonely who have tea in the afternoon, Georges/Gilles had said. Real people make love. Like this, my love, ma chérie. And he had bounded across the motel room towards the bed, just missed the window, and crashed into the wall. It had been difficult to get his shorts onto his inert body before she called the doctor. She was only thankful that the body was not lying on the sidewalk three floors below leaving her with impossible explanations to give to the police, to Robert, to her mother. And leaving Georges or Gilles with much more than a slight concussion and brief loss of memory.

Scarcely a day went by now without that little scene drifting through her mind like a float in a parade and prompting her to remember, tugging at her as if his name, recalled, spoken out, would be a clue to a better life. And lately she had a new fear of forgetting. Blanks in her mind could lead to connecting empty spaces, to scratched out data that could never be recovered, to oblivion.

Around her, the hum of voices continued.

She eats like a pig. Consolation perhaps. When I'm that age I'll come here for tea every day and eat six slices of cake.

The éclair was too rich. Cream and chocolate and heavy choux pastry. Forbidden fats. She dabbed at her mouth with the white linen napkin provided. Some people still did laundry. Standards were kept up here at the Ritz.

Le telephone sonne. Elle ne bouge pas. Tu le vois. Exactement.

The young man ate another sandwich hopefully, and, pushing her scarf out of the way, his friend leaned across the table to pour his tea for him.

That jacket, the woman in the corner, worth three thousand at least.

Two young women, perfect hair, perfect faces, still wearing summer dresses now at the end of September, sat at the table to her right, sipping their tea, eating nothing. Packages were stacked on the floor around them. Tennis tomorrow. Dancing tonight. *I have been you, looked like you. Well-kept and slim. Beware! Out there a man called Robert is waiting.*

A glow surrounded the young lovers on her left: She gathered her hair in her hand behind her head again, a nervous gesture, as she repeated, "Exactement." And he continued his tale, "Ce qu'elle a dit la prochaine fois."

That woman looks familiar. She's in here all the time.

Nothing else to do. Poor old thing. But that hair. The jacket.

Jeanne glanced round the room, so familiar. Blue and gold round the door, scenic oil paintings on the walls, trees, lakes, cabins in snow, nothing controversial. Discreet lighting. *The chill smile of luxury.* Like home. Like the homes of her friends. No fingermarks on the paint, no toys loosely lying around. "I would have liked children," she had once cruelly said to Robert. "Would they have liked you?" he had cruelly replied.

The player returned to the grand piano and began again to bring out those tunes of old loves lost and forgotten. Sweet notes dripped down on to the elaborate carpet. A few years ago, in bars that smelt of smoke and alcohol and sweat, she had spent time sitting beside pianos like that, drinking gin, making conversation. Welcomed because she knew the latest lines, knew how to make the customers laugh. Would hitch up her skirt when drunk, drape a scarf round her shoulders and huskily imitate the great Marlene. In the early hours, she could make them cry with "Das Lied ist aus."

The blonde at the table near the piano gave the waiter a sharp look.

In her own blonde period, Jeanne had cast looks like that around and for her pains had landed Maurice. "I love you," Maurice had shouted; he'd sent her flowers, chocolates, small pieces of furniture, and had nearly killed himself with a Chinese cabinet. *Something very special, sweetheart.* Impatient always, he couldn't wait for movers. He called a taxi and the taxi wasn't big enough. (This all came out later.) So he called for a station wagon taxi and he and the driver loaded the cabinet into it. And he insisted, though the driver was a strong young man, on carrying it up the flight of steps to her door. "I want to surprise her," were his near-last words. And he had. When she opened the door, he was gasping over the cabinet. Pale as dough, he slid slowly down onto the top step and rolled onto the street, the cabinet after him. "If," the doctor said, "the cabinet had landed on his head it would have been the end."

Why did they never love her gently?

A fairly fatal woman, Robert had called her. Une femme presque fatale. (Her lovers didn't die but their lives were often spoilt for a time.)

There were others who came to no harm, she had cried out in her own defence.

That woman's life is written in her hair. Was that what the young man at the next table said?

And what had Amelie to offer Robert that she had not offered, and offered more lovingly? She is young, Robert had said as if that was all that mattered.

"Your bill, Madame?"

"I'd like more hot water. No wait. I'll have a gin and tonic, Pierre."

"Mais certainement."

Students together, she and Robert, they had looked in this very window and laughed at bourgeois pretension and at waste. He would laugh now to see her munching on scones, spreading them with red currant jam although every sweet bite made her teeth ache. "I'm not enjoying this," she said under her breath to his ghost. Although, in fact, she was.

They had married furtively and spent the honeymoon writing leaflets in a glow of righteous activism. The world would know them, the world would change on their account. The starving would eat, the displaced would find homes, all that was wrong would be made right.

But the path had curved. Truth came out of the USSR. Idols fell. Exams were passed. Aims altered. Robert changed. He began to make money, liking it.

The fact of her life: "Men come to harm around you," he had said before he left her as if that and not the young Amelie was the reason for his leaving after thirty-seven years. He left her and caught pneumonia and died and left her all the money he had made. *Too bad, Amelie! No time to change the will.* Perhaps after all he had not forgotten all those years before her hair turned red when she had been unpaid secretary, slave, and general enticer of business partners. *You set me up, Robert!*

What do you think she did in life?

Ran a brothel!

Laughter.

Her face is familiar.

What are you doing here? she wanted to ask the young lovers at the next table. *What has happened to the world? Is it at peace? Is no one hungry? Is no one wrongfully imprisoned? Can mankind be left to itself while you have tea in here, in this lush place? Are there no leaflets to be written, no causes, no barricades!*

The pianist gave her a knowing look. He thought he knew all about her: She was written out before him like a sheet of music. As if she was still singing, doing her smoky-voiced impersonation, *It isn't by chance I happen to be, A femme fatale, the toast of Paris.* The others at the tables around her knew her too. She was the woman with red hair in the very expensive jacket. And they spelled out her life for her as she did theirs. They saw her future, were prescribing it for her. She could see it written on the rich walls. Tea at the Ritz, tea at the Ritz, on every page of her calendar from now until the handwriting tapered to a scrawl, tea at the R. . . . A final day not filled in.

A feeling that might be indigestion groped around her heart. A stirring disturbance. A scone too many. The last éclair. The feeling spread to her mind like the gathering winds of a tornado. Long-forgotten young ideas swirled in her head. She experienced a sudden cold hatred of the room around her: the red chairs, the icy paintings, the blue and gold paint, the old waiter who had never roused himself to rebel against his servitude. And out there, out there, the things that she and Robert had begun to do all those years ago were still undone.

At the window she saw a mass of hungry mouths, thin hands clawing at the glass, buildings on the other side of the street crumbled.

She heard a cry. Her own voice. They turned to look. Pierre and the young women and the blonde by the piano and the pianist. The young lovers and all the others in the room were turned towards her.

Were they expecting her to sing?

She looked back at the pianist. She was not going to sing for him again. Even though he pleaded. She was never again going to launch into *I'm new again* in a public place.

It was the knowing look in his eyes that made her do what she did next. He had never known her young, and yet he was presuming to know her whole life, future as well as past. He stared at her with condescending authority.

The sound had stopped. She understood that she had cried out. They were all still staring, waiting to see what she would do next.

His name wasn't Gilles or George. It was Jacques. Jacques. Recalling his name gave her power.

She stood up and undid the gold J on her collar and put it in her purse. Then she slipped the wonderful jacket off her shoulders, drew her arms out of the sleeves, and let it fall almost to the ground before she gathered it up with a flourish—just like a toreador.

Maurice had often told her she should be on the stage. *Can you see me, Maurice?*

She carried the jacket to the table where the young lovers were. With a slight bow, she handed the jacket to the girl and said, "You've been admiring this. Take it."

The girl's mouth formed the perfect oh of a scream as if she knew the menace of the jacket, that it could alter her whole young life and that she would be weighed down by all its implications. She pushed it away but Jeanne would not take it back. Pitiless, she left it half-draped over the young woman and marched to the exit. The waiter cruised over to the door to say to her, in English, "Is Madame feeling all right?"

"Madame is fine," she replied.

She put a fifty-dollar bill into his hand and said, "This is for you, Pierre. I don't think I'll be seeing you again, except perhaps through the window."

And she went out, down Sherbrooke, eastward, slowly at first, then gathering speed. Towards the university where she had met Robert in the first place.

The young man came running after her with the jacket in his hand, and as she turned to face him he drew back. This was not the face of the woman who had been wearing the jacket five minutes ago.

She ran and ran, away from him, away from the Ritz, away from their knowing looks, away from Robert who was dead. She ran faster than she knew she could. She had to keep on running because she was cool without her jacket and besides, she had no idea how far she had to go.

THE
COLONEL'S
WIFE

I don't normally cut the heads off other people's flowers—unless I'm provoked. Today it was the music that did it. Brought back the memory of it all. Vivid as pain. I'm not saying I'll dance because she's dead. I still can though. Forty years ago, I would have danced and sung and thrown a party. Now I'm having this little celebration on my own. Because she's dead. At last. The park is usually empty about this time. People eat dinner early here. So I can sit on this bench with my glass and my bottle and drink a little. Sing a song if I want. But not one of hers.

It's very foolish ever to be sure of anything. But when you're young you have a belief in the future and in yourself and in your lover too. Even maybe in your husband.

Geoffrey and I were married soon after he graduated from the Royal Military College. We stood together tall at the altar, everything perfect and fine—except for the flowers. The flowers were my sister's responsibility and she had them delivered to the house too early and left them out in all that heat. I've never known whether she did it on purpose, a kind of curse, because she'd wanted Geoffrey herself. Or whether it was just her careless way.

So there I was in this nine-hundred-dollar gown all white and lace holding bruised camellias. I tried to cradle them in my arms so they didn't show. Everything else WAS perfect. Even, for a time, Geoffrey.

The nine-hundred-dollar gown was one more thing my new Toronto in-laws had insisted on. In the Ottawa Valley in those days, we tailored expenditure to income with a sizable safety margin. We had sense. But his family had something to prove, I guess. Nine hundred dollars was a fortune in 1932. I'd come among people who set great store by appearance. To them, my Scottish ancestry was quaint and my ability to speak French was a drawback. He was the one who went to Paris. By the time I got there, decades later, the language had changed.

I met Geoffrey in Algonquin Park. I was on vacation. He was on leave. On the third date we began to cast words like *always* and *only* and *never* and *forever* around us like spells.

My family had a cottage. His family owned a wooden palace on an island. We walked in the woods. He gave me a token ring. A year later we had the big wedding. My family was overawed by his family's name and wealth. His mother looked as though she would break if you spoke sharply to her but was as tough as old boots.

My parents said I'd done well. My sister didn't speak to me for a year.

Year One of married life. Pictures still and moving go through my head: The dresses I wore. The ceremonies he took part in and I attended. The dahlias he grew in our garden in his brief spare time. He wasn't a demonstrative man, but I saw him once or twice stroking the petals of his dahlias and smiling to himself.

In Year Two he planted white Purity. His orange Magnificats flourished. The lavender Prime Ministers promised to be better next year. He allowed me to pick the bright pink Park Princess for the house.

Year Three: I was trying to get pregnant. He was trying to get promoted. Sometimes we worked as a team on one or the other. He was more successful. The youngest lieutenant became the youngest captain. He planted scarlet Red Imps.

Year Five: We had been posted to Royal Roads. We still had dahlias in the garden because when we moved he lifted the corms and packed them in labelled boxes. By now he was putting a lot more effort into his pet project than mine. We went to the right parties and entertained at our place and just about all the men I ever saw were in uniform. We danced and flirted. The Red Imps loved the climate. The new reddish orange Carmens flourished.

I tried to learn Spanish.

Year Seven: We were back in Ottawa. My mother wrote me off in favour of my sister who by then had three little darlings aged two and four and five. She joked about my wedding flowers whenever we met as if they had nothing to do with her. To my mother I was as barren as the Ottawa Valley in January. And of course it couldn't be dear Geoffrey's fault. He was a man! A man though who saw little chance of advancement if peace prevailed. He wanted, but never said, a chance to be heroic in a major way.

He took to having lunch with the editor of *Colour in Your Garden*.

Year Seven-and-a-Half: At last! War! He said goodbye to his dahlias. His life's work was about to be justified. He marched about the house getting ready to go as if to a military band. Where are my socks. Pom-pompom. Of course I love you. Pom-pom-pom. Look after the flowers. Pom-pom-pom. And everything in the garden was pink and white and gold. And purple. There were farewell ceremonies which he took part in while I watched.

Year Nine: The letters came. They were sweet and more sentimental than I'd expected. Darling Bluey, (He called me that, short for Blue Eyes, until the awfulness began. I used to say, after the divorce, that he didn't pay me alimony. He paid me acri-money.), how I miss your sweet morning face. Your loving arms. Your tender breasts. PS Don't forget to water the dahlias.

And I did water them. I talked to them, cherished them. There I was, for the first time in my life, alone. I had time. I organised OWAH, Officers' Wives at Home. And we gave aid and comfort to the returning wounded. In some cases more comfort was given than aid. It was a treat to some of them to come and see the flowers in the garden and have coffee. I baked a lot of muffins.

In the late Fall, according to orders, I dug the tubers up and put them out to dry in the sun. Next day I dipped them in just melted wax to store them till next year. Each spring I planted the dahlias out three feet apart. They were in full bloom when the Army of Liberation rode into Paris.

His next letter said, Bluey, (no darling, this time), I got it! You've probably seen it by now in the paper. I know I would never have achieved this without you. I've been given a new driver, a woman, very efficient. And to celebrate we went to a concert, a victory concert given by Maurice Chevalier and Marlene Dietrich. He sang "Every Little Breeze Seems to Whisper Louise." She sang "Falling in Love Again." She came to dinner with us afterwards.

He signed that letter, Colonel Geoff. The full title underlined. No kisses. Only stars.

I wrote back, Darling how wonderful, all you've worked for, well-deserved. We'll truly celebrate when you return. And I signed it with my real name. It was our twelfth wedding anniversary. I grew up. Goodbye Bluey. Hello Caroline.

I didn't get a letter then for two months.

But a glossy magazine, not one I ever bought myself, was dropped through the mail slot one day, the corner of page thirty-six turned down. Delivered by one of those people who always want you to know the truth. I suspected the wounded air force captain from Edinburgh who had been admiring my hair and eyes.

It was a clear picture. Very close up. Colonel Geoffrey smiling like a cat after cream and HER with that Mona-Lisa-on-the-loose look. Seen together leaving a restaurant. Or a hotel. The background didn't make it clear.

I went into the garden and cut the heads off his pompons and hybrids and thought about Josephine Bonaparte.

It was weird for a while, peace. The life that had become so unpredictable was about to return to what we had always thought was normal. There were shifting attitudes. Certain undefined fears. The Officers'

Wives at Home meetings took on the angry air of a therapy group. It was as if a new enemy was about to invade. But they were conquering heroes, weren't they? They were our loved ones. Weren't they?

He returned home suddenly, hollow like a man who has lost something. Not an arm or a leg but maybe the chance of another kind of life. His uniform was grand with gold braid, and that gave him satisfaction. He held me in his arms, but I knew he was looking over my shoulder into the distance.

When he saw the dahlia stalks he went berserk. For the next few months, he played her records to himself and sometimes I think he cried.

His third wife is someone very like me, they say. I came to live here, in Vancouver. The climate's softer and I was able to get work as a fundraiser with Music International. My wartime experience paid off.

On our silver wedding anniversary, I gave myself a little holiday. I drove onto the ferry, sailed across the Strait and went to the place he'd retired to on the Island, near Victoria. There were toys on the grass, a swing. Dahlias growing in a big crescent-shaped bed. It was dusk. Neither of his children was in the yard that day. Not the boy. Not the girl who died young. I kept the biggest head for years, dried, under glass. People see him as a tragic figure.

My sister moved in with me three years ago. That's why I had to come out here to have my celebration. She's never been a drinker. And when I stagger a little she thinks it's my arthritis acting up and tries to be kind. After our divorce, Geoffrey married the editor of *Colour in Your Garden*. It only lasted a year. She came to a violent end. I didn't go to the funeral.

All day on the radio they've been playing her music. Marlene's. Paying homage.

When he was over there in Paris I think he imagined himself a Peter, a Johnny, one of the ones she sang those words to. He didn't understand that to her, he was just another no-name soldier.

I would always have called him Geoffrey.

I didn't mean to cut off quite so many heads today. But to me dahlias still have the insolent look of glossy faces in a magazine. When you've had faith in something, when you've gone along thinking that what you had was pure gold and it turns out to be tin, it eats into you, drives you a little mad. You can't help yourself.

The city gardener will come to work in the morning and see the bare stalks. He'll think it was vandals. There'll be a column in the paper about how destructive young people are these days, and maybe a picture.

The evening people are beginning to come into the park now. Two very young lovers. Five kids with a football. The old man who likes to watch the young lovers. A plain-clothes policeman looking for drug dealers. A pretty young woman in green striped leggings being dragged along by a German Shepherd.

My sister can't get her own dinner. She relies on me. Her three little darlings aged fifty-five and fifty-seven and fifty-eight lead busy lives elsewhere. She'll be calling my name.

Time to go. To pack up. My coat has deep pockets. They hold everything an old woman like me needs: A bottle. A glass. A knife.

A
TOAST
TO
LIFE

Alarm bells were ringing, and fragments of love songs broke through Jo's morning dream. Demons dispersed. Her mother's voice told her that it was time to get up. The voice on the radio told her that true love was rare. She put one foot out of bed and touched the floor. A reality check.

She chose her clothes with care. Green-striped leggings, loose purple sweater looped with gold thread, scarf embracing those colours and edged in red. It wasn't the day for plain clothes.

In the kitchen her mother was making a dip with seven layers, guacamole, refried beans, grated cheddar, salsa, sour cream, chopped eggs, caviar on top. A special treat to go with the fancy breads she had bought yesterday. The fridge was half full of white wine.

"Mom!"

"Well it's a very special day, honey. And it's not a lot of trouble, really."

She was chopping hard-cooked eggs to make the

third layer although, she said, some people put the eggs just below the caviar, like to like.

"It's not a big deal, Mother."

"It's your first film, dear. And I want to do this. Let me be proud. Please."

Jo owned no weapons to smash the grip her mother still had on the events of her life. She wished she could watch the film alone in an enclosed box. Her mother and Sue and Marge and the others would never understand what she was trying to say. They would see the images but make no connection. Their comments would be to endure. And at the end, after they had said *wonderful, really good*, one of them would add, *Well it's clever, dear, but I'm not sure I know what it means*.

Unspoken would be surprise that this nice child, nice child of a nice home, could know and say such awful things.

"I'll spread some of this egg on toast for you. You shouldn't go to work hungry."

"No thanks."

"Eat something, Joanne."

She walked out, almost skipping, *this is mydaymydaymyday*, down the slope of the street towards the centre of the city. She lifted her feet off the sidewalk hardly noticing them touch the cement.

The sky was a determined blue, the clouds were like meringue, music flowed from open windows, and sunlight bounced off the beige walls of the mall. It was a perfect morning. People on the sidewalk were staring upward watching a body tumble from the roof of Eaton's, its arms and legs flailing outwards, grasping nothing. Emergency vehicles with strange designs on them wailed their way towards the body the moment it touched ground.

Jo waited for them to pass before she crossed the road. This day was like a stamp on her passport to the future. The justification of four years spent writing, ignoring her friends, buying cameras, living at home, being twenty-seven.

She imagined herself in Hollywood, but had reservations. Did she want, did she really want, to be there lost in those canyons, working amongst bigger, longer names like Tarantino and Spielberg? A dream of fame based on a half-hour video about the violence of a city! After every showing, the credits would flash up on the screen, black on white. *Produced and directed by Joanne Krause.* At the last minute she had changed the title from "Urban Life" to "Urban Death."

The emergency vehicles were waved away and the lifeless heap on the sidewalk was hauled to one side.

"Hey Jo!"

"Hi Tom! How's it going?"

"The dummy's too light. They should add weight. Want a sandwich?"

"No thanks. 'Urban Death' is on tonight. 7:30."

"I heard. Beginning eh?"

"I guess so."

Four years ago at UBC they had both seen the movie world as an Aladdin's cave for which they might never have the password. Now they were inside it able to see and touch the glittering jewels. Touch but not yet pry loose.

Tom said, "They've been putting Prozac in the popcorn. Audiences are ruminating. These guys know that.

They're going to let the dummy go down light again. Can you believe it!"

The passers-by were still looking up, mouths agape, as if they hoped a live actor might be thrown off the roof for the sake of realism and give them a chance to be present at a true tragedy. *Do you know what I saw today, honey!*

"I'll be watching," Tom called after her.

She turned her back on the scene and looked at the distant ocean, deceptively peaceful. For her next film she would use clips of the war in Somalia, Rwanda, Bosnia. How could they, the TV viewers of the world, understand evil unless their faces were pushed into heaps of rotting corpses? How many of them were like her mother, like Sue and Marge and Harriet, only intent on making life around them pleasant?

At Reception, Gloria, with her false red hair, sixty-nine if a day, was crying.

"Marlene touched us all with glamour," she said, sniffling. "She was part of my history. And why does she want to be buried there?"

"Don't cry, Gloria."

"I have to express myself, Joanne, if you please."

Jo wanted to say sorry but Gloria, indignant through her tears, turned back to the switchboard.

"They're waiting for you in C," Gloria called after her.

"A man threw himself off the top of Eaton's," Jo said in the studio, testing the sound.

Alec dabbed at her face with powder. She straightened her scarf and waited.

"Ready in five."

"Two minutes of you as a kind of intro," Howard said. "And try not to be morbid."

"I'm not Pollyanna."

"Just smile, we'll do the rest."

"I'm supposed to talk. I mean it's my film."

"Nothing belongs. So smile."

She smiled.

"Give us a few words. Your thoughts on why you felt compelled to make this rather nasty short film. And keep it clean."

"With all the killing in the world," she said, and could see Howard rolling his eyes, "I wanted to make a statement about the way we ignore the violence around us. We get smug. Today, here in downtown Vancouver, a man was thrown off the top of Eaton's."

"Come on Joanne. We're wasting time here."

"I'm not kidding."

"Now!"

"*Urban Death* is a movie about our habit of standing by allowing all kinds of killing to go on in other parts of the world just because the people are of another race, speak another language. And it begins here. People are run down and the driver drives on. People are battered and no one intervenes."

She gave them her two minutes of anger and knew that they were looking at her sideways and sticking labels on her: Young! Bright but needs new ideas.

In her office she picked up a message from Harold Stengle. *Congratulations. Looking forward. Send video.* Next week she could maybe ask for a bigger office. Two of the actors called to say they were nervous, how was she? "Fine," she told them. "Just fine. And you were great."

She turned to other people's scripts, her daily bread. *Dear writer, we have now read 'Supermarket Werewolf' and while it is well-written we cannot fit it into our schedule in the near future.*

Later, as she walked back through the square, an explosion hit the street and shook the air around her. Another villain blown to smithereens, fragments dripping down like bloody rain. People kept back by yellow tape gasped at the wreckage of a real car smoking in the street. A car they might have liked to own, destroyed for entertainment.

Jo wanted to shoo them away, send them back to their lives. Tom waved.

"Good luck," he said.

"Thanks, Tom."

"Now they've made too much blood. I'm going into cartoons after this. At least with imaging you can get it right. You have control."

Jo bumped into a man carrying flowers, holding them out in front of him as if he was allergic to them, roses, carnations, fern.

"Sorry," she said. "I hope I haven't crushed them."

But the man, no doubt on his way to see his mother, moved quickly on.

At the real estate office, the agent merely shook his head at her: Nothing in your price range right now. Call again next week.

Two cops were running through the curved doorway of the Blue Palm. Early in the day for a fight. She walked on and from an open basement window she heard the deep voice singing, "'Underneath the lamplight, by the barrack square.'"

And a man shouted, "That's not her singing. It's a man. It's a man's song!" The window slammed down.

Her mother was still in the kitchen, perhaps had been there all day long. Now she was cutting raw carrots into neat, even sticks.

"Your cousin Kim didn't get to Yugoslavia after all. She's somewhere in Europe travelling with that woman from the office. I don't know why they don't go for real holidays. It drives Myra crazy. Do you realise this is the anniversary of the day the war ended? They might have filled the whole of prime time with that, you know."

For the showing of her next film, Jo would send out for trays of prosciutto and melon, crates of Puilly-Fuissé, and the guests would admire the view from a balcony overlooking the Strait.

"And why she always has to go with that Sharon. I know her mother worries."

"Mother. Women go on vacation together all the time. It's safer. They have more fun."

"I'd like you to have a boyfriend. It's only natural at your age."

"Film-makers only have time for their art," she replied. "And you waited till you were thirty-five."

They both laughed.

"How many people for Chrissake?"

"Only five. You could have invited your friends too. I told you."

"Next time, Mom."

The women arrived promptly at 7:15 so as to be sitting down before the program began. Jo looked at their faces. Sue hanging on to youth, flexible enough still to sit on the floor. Marge, her mother's old neighbour from the first house, finding a chair that was good for her back. Harriet, older than all of them but working still, looking for comfort. They had come to watch their friend's daughter's film. Out of loyalty. Out of a kind of love. They had much to say. Always. To each other. But now they were giving their attention to her.

It's just a short feature, she wanted to say. *You won't like it.*

They fell into their habit of instant chat, prescripted. How is he now? What did you say when she? Have you had the house painted yet? Did you like the covers? Jen and Barb are late as usual.

Mother said, "Everyone got a drink?"

Sue said, "Success at last."

Harriet nodded.

Her mother said, "It makes up for everything."

Joanne looked at her and wondered what 'everything' embraced. Too much perhaps, like the seven-layer dip. All different colours and textures. But now her six months' work was about to be justified. Six months! Much longer if you counted getting it together, getting studio time, persuading Rashid that it wouldn't harm his reputation to help with the editing. Though at the end he wanted no credit, he had told her it was good, something to be pleased with. A fine beginning.

Her mother turned up the sound. The first notes of music came out of the box into the room. Strange chords. A husky voice began to sing, "Falling in love again."

Jo jumped up. "That's not what I used. I'll kill them. It had to be new. This isn't right. They've changed everything."

And then, white across the screen, the tiny dots formed letters to spell out: Regular programming has been pre-empted so that we can present a tribute to Marlene Dietrich who died in Paris yesterday at the age of ninety-four.

Her mother said, "Well now. Well."

There were murmurs, and Sue in her yellow dress said, "They'll show it again, dear."

Sympathy. Kindness. Enough to wallow in. Joanne looked round at them, all these older women, and hated them for their comfort. Most of them were turning back to the screen, pleased that they would hear old songs, responding to a dead old woman's life. That woman meant something to them. They knew her. She had been part of their time.

"You can show us the video, darling," her mother said softly. "Later."

There were less interested murmurs from the others as a clip from an old movie, a scene in a bar, the star in a short, short skirt, appeared on the screen.

"We'll do this again on Wednesday."

"Maybe at my house," Sue said. "I'll make lemon pie. You used to love my lemon pie when you were little, Joanne."

They were gathering her in, offering her support, their kind of love, taking their eyes from the screen for a moment to show they cared.

"I'll take the dog out," she cried. "It's all right."

She ran from them and from their affection. They were old. They had lived their lives. What did they know now! They spent their time decorating their comfortable nests, reassuring each other that they were alive. They had come to terms.

Perce, shut in the kitchen, greeted her with joy. She got his leash, and he followed her out of the back door and pulled her to the park. "All right, all right," she said to him, "we'll go and look at the sea."

The park was deserted at that hour. Mother said never to go there alone in the evening. Even in daylight. It was the quiet time. A few kids were pushing a ball about. A man and woman were entwined, this perhaps their only meeting place. Empty stalks reared up in the flowerbed. A city gardener gone mad?

From a little way off she heard a murmuring sound, a familiar tune, as if the broadcast she had run away from had followed her. The sounds became notes, became a song. She tried to make out words and heard, "'You say Auf wiedersehen but you think, Good riddance.'"

She turned the corner and saw a figure on a bench, very still, sitting alone. An elderly woman. There was lace under the coat. A touch of it. A gold and black scarf shone round her neck, and the coat, long and pleated, tiny accordion pleats, was clearly expensive. There was a bottle beside her on the bench. Dark green, gold top. Champagne. A cut-glass flute. Looking off into the centre for a full shot, the old woman stopped singing and poured herself a drink with care, set the bottle down and lifted the glass to her lips. Then she held the glass out towards some invisible friend or perhaps even to her God in a gesture of celebration.

Jo looked for lights, for a camera crew, for a director. But there was no one. Only the old woman on her bench on this May evening, drinking a private toast.

Perce pulled her on, but Jo held him back and stayed to watch as the woman put the bottle and the glass into the inner pockets of her lovely raincoat. "Poachers' pockets" her grandmother would have called them. The woman had a definite air about her as if she had been in command of something, of her own life at least. Jo wanted to follow her to ask what it was that she celebrated alone. A birthday? A renewal of love? A fortune? The safe recovery of a loved one? Survival? Instead, she accepted the mystery as a gift. A story to be created later.

She led Perce slowly back to the house. She was determined to be polite, to be nice, to tell her mother's friends she would show them the video at Sue's house on Wednesday. And that she still loved lemon pie.

Her mother was sitting alone in the kitchen, tears running down her cheeks.

"Mom, I'm sorry."

"It's not you, Joey."

From the other room, loudly, came the unique voice singing another man's song: *Who is standing beside you by the lamppost now?* asks the soldier on the front line of hell. Jo followed her mother for a moment into that world, the world of death and apocalypse and lost lives and lost people.

"I'm here," she said.

Her mother reached out for her hand and dabbed her eyes and said, "We'd better go back to the others."

The others were singing softly, along with their dead idol. The music had taken on the holy sound of a hymn. The room was full of ghosts and dark memories.

Joanne shivered. And then, as far as she knew the words, she joined in their song.

When they asked her what her next film was to be, she would tell them it had to do with courage. And it would begin with the image of a woman drinking champagne alone in the park, drinking a toast to life.

THE
VIOLET
BED

Ellie said, "The cornflowers are out." They were dwarfs, stunted flowers no more than twelve centimetres high but they were the stunning lapis lazuli blue of the full-sized blooms. A sign, she said every year, of summer.

"Happy Birthday, sweetheart," Ted said. They had long ago forsworn cards and gifts. Big companies had turned anniversaries into retail events that had more to do with greed than love. Sitting opposite her, he poured granola into his bowl, the rough brown bowl she'd made specially for him in her first pottery class. He added half a banana evenly sliced and passed the other half to her. Goat's milk stood between them in its flowered jug. Soon she would look up and say *paradise* and he would reply, *heaven*.

It was their currency.

And this was the way they had chosen to live. Sixteen years ago they had moved to the cottage, four of them then. He and Ellie had planned out a life which included as a matter of fact, non-negotiable, that they would remain in love forever. And when the other two had left, unable to endure the seclusion, he and Ellie had been delighted to have the house and the land to themselves.

They'd needed no binding ceremony to proclaim that they were each other's for eternity. Their love would not be a selfish inward thing but would radiate out to the world, giving the world a small glow, making one small part of it a better place.

Three days a week he drove twenty-two kilometres to work in the fish plant near Nanaimo. On Fridays and Saturdays, she drove thirty-one kilometres in the other direction to sell homemade bread and cake in the market at Chemainus. Thursdays and Sundays were their own shared time. To talk, to tend the garden, to read and sculpt and paint. He was working on a large canvas depicting lovers on a river bank. It had started out a year ago as a post-impressionist idyll, but lately the shadows of the trees had grown darker and the eyes in the foliage were no longer of birds but of demons, and when he stood in front of it alone, he wanted to back away.

Two of his smaller works had sold well nine years ago just after Pat and Marie-France had left. With the proceeds he bought the green pickup. Now we're in clover, Ellie had said. And Ted had tried not to let himself dwell on the idea that clover was for bees and ruminants.

The phone rang, irritating them both. It was the woman who'd moved into the place down the lane inviting them to join a protest march. *Save the salmon, save the trees, save the park.* This time it was to save a tiny island in the Gulf.

Ted handed the receiver to Ellie.

"We don't join protests," she said. And she had to go on and explain that they were caring for their three acres in their own way, living a plastic-free life and working on sustainable development. People who knew them no longer asked for their support.

After a pause, he heard Ellie say, "Really? I thought she died years ago."

When she'd put the receiver down, she turned to him and said, "Marlene Dietrich is dead."

"Oh," he replied. "Oh." As if there was some undefined pain for him in the news. As if a family friend had died. His grandfather had boasted of meeting the star once in New York. It had been the bright moment of Grandad's life, to hear him talk. Ted's mother had loved her movies and envied her legs. And he'd grown up conscious of a well-lit profile and the shimmering voice of a sexy older woman. He felt tears rise to his eyes and a sob in his throat. He turned away. How could the death of an old singer make him cry? What was she to him! He took a deep breath and wondered if he was becoming allergic to the smell of yeast.

"She was pretty old," Ellie said.

"Pretty old," Ted repeated.

"You're doing it," Ellie mocked.

Last weekend Ellie's sister had made one of her short visits, stopping by on her way from a meeting in Victoria. "Bottom line" and "product" were her words. Grass and trees were no more than scenery to her. She changed the atmosphere in the house as if she brought pollution with her, droplets and dust of angry city life. As she was leaving to catch the ferry from Nanaimo, she'd said, "You two talk with one mind, which would

be cute if you were six-year-old twins. It's beginning to
sound ridiculous. Your hair is turning grey."

Ellie had turned on her sister and told her that she'd
always been envious and it was a pity she couldn't
spend a week or two with them and feel the effect of
truly harmonious living. Gemma called a cab and
wouldn't let Ted drive her to Nanaimo in the truck. On
Sunday evening they drank Gemma's gift of wine and
wished her enlightenment.

"Are you feeling better this morning, love?" Ellie
asked now.

Ted had explained away last evening's torpor by
saying that the fish truck stank and the office itself was
beginning to make him ill: They kept the windows
closed and Boris smoked and they had taken him out
for a beer or two at lunch. Soon, given the rising price
of even their cost of living, he would have to start working a regular week. Five days. But he would have to look
for something different.

"Did you see anyone?" Ellie asked.

They always asked each other that. Like notes delivered in cleft sticks to missionaries in remote parts
of Africa long ago, conversation with others brought
news from the outer world.

"Only the guys at work," he said. "But I heard that
Marie-France is moving back to Sidney."

"Really?"

And then, foolishly, he went into more detail than
was natural.

"She's got fed up with the gallery. With Vancouver.
Wants to work on her own. Take on a partner maybe.

And branch out a little. Her parents left her something. She can afford to buy a building. Probably. I mean I'm guessing that."

"Oh," Ellie said. She poured him half a cup of coffee from the thermos that held their day's ration.

"Is she still with him?"

"I don't think so," he answered, recalling Marie-France's tears and his own embrace.

"They never had faith in the plan. She and Pat. When they left here, I thought we'd never see them again. I hope she won't expect to visit. She's too earthy for me. There has to be a belief in beauty. In the eternal. It was when she suggested that we . . ."

"Yes," he said to cut her off, not wanting to be reminded of a scenario that even after nearly a decade, aroused him when he thought about it.

Marie-France had met him coming out of the video store yesterday. He was carrying *six videos for ten dollars for one week. Special offer.*

"You two still living life on the small screen?" she had said and led him to Cafe Arabica for a latte and a croissant and after that to the hotel for a drink.

He was late back at the office, but Boris had only smiled at him and nodded. And Ted had smiled and nodded back at Boris.

"I'm beginning to hate the smell of fish," he said.

"'Hate' darling?" Ellie looked at him over the top of her glasses.

"Sorry."

He pulled a dollar from his pocket and put it into the red china pig on the table.

"If that pig ever gets full," she said.

He picked it up and shook it.

"About thirty more years, I should think."

Ellie was wearing her Thursday sweater. It was patched at the sleeve where the puppy had grabbed it. Her face was smooth. Her eyes clear. For all those years of love-making, she looked untouched, virginal, and he couldn't help at times resenting that. Sometimes though, she looked wise beyond reason as if there was something about her that he could never know. But then her eyes caught his, and he knew she was going to say, "Love like ours is rare."

And she did. She drew a heart in the air with her finger and struck an arrow through it. He blew her a kiss. Later she would wash lentils and make a stew with last year's carrots and beans. At dinner he would make a salad, cabbage and radishes, oil and vinegar.

It was all so simple. She had chosen him. He had chosen her. They had made various vows such as never to have children. Not because, as some of their friends said, there were too many in the world and a lot of them neglected, but because their twin plans of life-and-art and life-as-art precluded children. The dogs absorbed her motherliness and he loved the quiet that surrounded them like an eggshell.

Often, returning along the dirt road to the house in those years, he'd been aware of driving into a kind of haven which was perhaps sinful in its deep felicity. And for which someone, sometime, would demand payment. Now and then he felt afraid.

She came to his side of the table and put her arms round him. She smelt of ginger and pineapple. The bath oil was her one extravagance. Her voice in all these years hadn't aged at all. It was the full high tone of a very young woman.

"I'm going to weed the veggies. Could you take Dief for a walk after you've done the bed?"

Ted put his dish in the sink to wait there till evening when they would wash the whole day's collection at once, and went to the bedroom.

His head still ached, and he felt like lying down. He wanted to spend one day doing nothing at all, a day when he was free to think nothing and most particularly to admire nothing. But he folded the duvet back to air the futon and shook the pillows. They were still using the covers they'd been given as a kind of leaving-the-world gift by her mother. And Ellie had dyed them violet because Ted once said they were his favourite flower.

In the early years they had, on Thursdays and Sundays, spent hours making love and drinking wine. But wine had gone the way of cards and presents. Occasional gifts were welcomed and drunk quickly. And when Ted met a friend from the old days in Nanaimo, he found he could drink a whole bottle easily.

He called out "Dief!" And both dogs came towards him with slow excitement. The old fellow was weary and needed exercise to help his bowels and his arthritic joints. The puppy pranced round yapping.

"Not too far," Ellie shouted. "And don't let Prince follow. He'll go too fast."

Ted took hold of the terrier and pushed him into the back shed. "Prison for you, Prince." And closed the door. He attached the metal clip of the leash to the old dog's collar and set off slowly through the trees at the end of the garden, the spot where the hammock had

hung when they were both slim enough to lie in it together.

He looked at the notch round the tree trunk made
by the rope. There she had trailed her hand on the
grass, her body touching his to madness till they had
rolled out of the hammock and made love on the earth,
unseen in their private place. Sometimes they had lain
still for hours, their souls in perfect harmony. Hand in
hand, looking up at the sky, scarcely aware of there
being a world at all. Enclosed in true communion, they
needed no drugs to take them into a sphere of existence known only to the chosen. They had defined ecstasy.

He looked back and Ellie was there in the garden,
waving. He moved out of sight through the trees. He
talked to the reluctant dog, asking it how they could go
on as they were. The dog only panted in reply. He
heard Ellie's voice as if she was calling to him to come
back but shut his ears and went on, letting his life run
backwards through his mind. Back to school, to his
remote mother, his might-have-been father, Grandad's
stories a running stream of words in the background
of their days.

He began to walk faster. Dief whined, protesting. But
Ted was unable to stop himself, his legs were a force
on their own. He was moving at speed through scenery he had once loved. Or was some cinematic mira-
cle moving the trees on either side of him while he and
the dog stood still? He became less and less aware of
leaves and bark and birds and the quick breath of the
tired animal. Trees got taller and sunlight filtered onto
the path ahead of him grudgingly, piece by piece.

The dog had stopped whining but was dragging,

dragging him back. Trying to drag him back. He pulled it on and on, unable to stay still, possessed by some demon. The demon in his head that was telling him a truth he hadn't dared to face. Flashing it before him like a series of cue cards. Telling him that while he had life and years left, he must get away from the enchanted garden. *Get away from her. Away from her. From her. Her.*

"Hate!" he shouted at the top of his voice. "Hate!" And then began to laugh. He sat down on a tree stump and put his head on his hands. Weeping for her sorrow but weeping for his own joy. The dog lying beside him on the grass appeared to be in perfect sympathy with him, a look of wise agreement on its simple face.

"Dief. Dief," Ted said. "Lives change. There is progress."

In response, the dog closed its eyes. Ted gave him time to recover and then pulled him to his feet. They'd been out for an hour. She'd be worried. Yes, she would be worried. The thought struck him that she tied him to her with bonds of time. Marie-France had said, "She will get over it. You both need to be free. It will be better for her too. In time, if you go on like this, you will hate each other."

Ellie was older than he but not old. She too perhaps wanted a chance at life but had been afraid to say. She had once or twice mentioned that she might like to move from clay to stone, if there was space, if there was time. He would offer her the best birthday gift of all: Freedom from bonds, the chance of renewal, a whole new beginning. *Not that we need part forever*, he would say. *We've had too much for that. But life is opportunity. Life is for making plans. Now. Before we get old. There should be more than one bright moment in a man's life.*

Full of new energy, he tried to run but the dog held him back. Finally, he picked Dief up and carried him, able to take long strides in spite of the weight.

Ellie was no longer in the garden. He stepped into the kitchen to offer her a different way of life. *We can't go on living out of the world,* he would say. *There are people out there, there are new ideas, there are other places. Our time for seclusion is over.*

He set his burden down gently and called out her name.

Ellie came into the room carrying two mugs of coffee.

"You've been," she began to say but saw his face and read the look in his eyes and stopped still. She screamed and the mugs of coffee fell to the floor.

Then she saw the dog. Blood was oozing from Dief's mouth. Twigs and leaves clung to his fur.

Without another word, she went across the hall to their bedroom. And returned.

Silently she covered the animal with a mauve pillowslip.

Silently she lifted the corpse and carried it to the deck. Silently she came back into the house, closing the door behind her. As she moved across the room towards Ted, she kicked the shards of pottery aside.

Ellie loved the evening. May. The sun going down over the hills, touching the tops of the fir trees with gold and orange light. Often they'd stood on the little deck, enjoying a glass of wine in those days when they'd been able to afford it. He preferred red. She liked a good Italian white. Glass in hand, arms twined, bringing the glasses to their mouths they drank each other in. One day, and how they had lied to explain it to the doctor, he'd tripped and his glass had struck her lip. His tears. Her blood. Her pain. His comfort. The scar remained like a love-bite from a sadistic lover.

Those evenings had not lost their glow when the wine had become apple juice and occasionally, in a month when there had been too many holidays, water.

Their love had not faltered. They had agreed on forever, a forever that was true and non-negotiable. When their hands met an electric current had run between them. They'd joked that they could supply power to a small town with their passion.

She sang as she worked, the Dionne Warwick song they'd both liked, "'I'll never love like this again.'"

She shovelled rhythmically. Her muscles had become stronger over time from lifting dogs, hefting thirty-kilogram bags of kibble or sacks of flour from the truck to the house. She didn't care that dirt and pebbles were falling in a shower on to the cornflowers. She put the spade into the ground, pushed it down and forward, then lifted and threw. Up and over. When the hole was deep enough she stood in it and dug from the sides. She would plant herbs over the mound perhaps, or violets, which had been his favourites. A bed of violets for remembrance and, for economy and usefulness, a small apple tree to send down roots into his body and provide fruit. A monument to sustainable growth.

IN
MOVIES

In old movies HE, or SHE herself, reached round and took a pin out of HER hair and it fell round HER shoulders and made HER instantly beautiful. Plain to glamorous in one instant. The one pin had often held back a Niagara of hair.

In five years of working for the same company, Bertrand Greene never touched Inge Johansson and certainly had never tried to reach round her head to pull off the elastic bow that held back her long braid. *Good morning,* he usually said. *What's moving today? I'm going to be away this afternoon. If my wife calls* . . .

For the first three years at Bryden, she had been Bertrand's secretary, and he had often introduced her to others as "Ms. Speed and Accuracy," as though swift fingers and an eye for errors made up for a lack of glamour. In that scenario, she was supposed to smile and nod and look coyly down at her keyboard. Now that she was assistant manager, and her office was next to his, he spoke to her about prospects, about clients, about stocks and rising companies. He valued her clear view of the money market.

In her time, Bertrand Greene had seduced fourteen women that Inge knew of and many more that she didn't. *Write to me at the office, darling,* he said to them. He obviously said to them. Because letters came to him. Several a week. He kept them in a box in the bottom right-hand drawer of his desk. Inge was depressed by the sameness of them, their lack of variety. They revealed, more than anything, the banality of lust.

She was first at the office most days, and after she'd taken off her coat and changed her shoes she put on the coffee pot and enjoyed the first fresh cup before Cathy and Janice and all the others arrived. It was a moment when the whole fifteenth floor of the building belonged to her. She could stroll over to the window and see the city spread around below her and know that it too was hers: The skyscrapers and roads, the trees just coming out, the few old buildings not yet fallen victim to development. For that brief time her real estate assets amounted to much more than a one-bedroom apartment at the end of the subway line and an eventual fifth share in the family farmhouse.

It was also her chance to be alone with the mail. This morning, among the subscription notices, the letters from clients pleased or irate, from societies, from companies promoting mines that had been idle for years, sales offering tremendous bargains, there were three hand-written envelopes addressed to Bertrand Greene. Two of them were from older women who had been writing to him for a year or more. The handwriting on the third envelope was also familiar.

It was a morning for tea. Inge plugged in the kettle and put a tea bag in her mug. She put coffee into the machine for the others and turned it on. *Bless you, Inge,* they would say, when they came in and found the coffee ready. They treated her with affection, seeing her as non-threatening, if over-efficient. She was sure that at times they referred to her as "poor Inge" and did not care.

The kettle began to boil and she held the letter, flap-side down, in the steam and opened the envelope. The paper too was familiar. It was the kind she had given to Marilyn last Christmas. Blue paper with pansies in one corner.

Dearest, dearest B.

What can I say? What an evening. The wine! And when you compared us to a shipwrecked couple, I knew it was right. I love you, you said to me. And did you mean it? You proved your love for me and I'm saying, did you mean it? I'm sorry, B. but how can I believe that you would move out of your lovely house and leave your wife? For me?

Inge, murmuring, idiot, idiot, looked at the signature hoping she was wrong.

I do believe, believe me. Marilyn.

So it was Marilyn! Marilyn, laughing, had said last Friday: *I can't make it to the movies, this week, Inge.* And on Tuesday: *I'd love to have lunch but I've got to get these papers across town.* And Marilyn knew! Together they had talked of Bertrand's loves and called him the lean Greene sex machine. She had fallen for his line. Marilyn had gone right out of her mind.

"Have you got my letters, Inge?" He was standing in front of her with his hand held out.

"You're early, Bertrand."

"I wish you'd leave the letters out there. It's Janice's job to sort them."

"I like to get a start." She handed him the others and kept the one from Marilyn in her hand, scrunched up, below the desk.

She gave him her usual good-morning-Bertrand smile and took in the splendour of his outfit. He was wearing the blue suit with the faint grey stripe, a blue shirt with a white collar, and a tie that was softly pink and purple. Discreet. Attractive.

He smiled back at her and said, "Your face is red."

"Just a touch of hay fever."

"Oh!"

It sounded like "Ugh." Damp eyes, a runny nose, hair drawn back from her face, tied not pinned at the nape of her neck. That was how he saw her. She knew that. He turned and went to his own office to read the day's catch. She straightened out the letter and read it again before she stuffed it into her purse. Oh Marilyn!

Before she moved to Foden and Kline, Marilyn had worked at Bryden Investments for seven years in Personnel. She had helped Inge to settle in, and they had discovered a mutual interest in old movies. Lately, they'd been enjoying the Dietrich revival at the Roxy. They had gone to the rerun of *Destry Rides Again*, sat twice through *Morocco*, and taken out the video of *The Blue Angel* to watch at home. Every week they went to a restaurant for lunch and talked over the new releases. But last Tuesday, Inge had eaten lunch at the Café du Marché alone.

Bertrand began to come to work early. The morning lost its magic for Inge. He gathered his mail and went into his office and closed the door, shutting her out. Inge went to see *Knight Without Armour* on her own but it was no fun, not having Marilyn there to talk it over and decide whether Dietrich had slept with Donat before or after the movie was made. She didn't even bother to go and see *The Devil is a Woman*. When the new Meryl Streep opened at the Revue, Inge asked Janice if she would like to go with her, but Janice had a live-in lover and was not yet independent.

The second weekend in June, to her parents' surprise, Inge went home to Ridgeville. She walked around the edge of the cornfield and touched the green shoots which were already knee-high. She wandered round the orchard under the falling blossoms and knew she would have to come back in August to help her mother gather in the fruit. At dinner she said little and only ate one piece of the pie that was made with last year's Montmorency cherries. When asked her opinion of the new shade of green on the kitchen walls, she had to admit she hadn't noticed it. Her mother, standing at the sink, cloth in hand, asked if she was pregnant.

On Sunday evening when he drove her to the bus station in St. Catharines, her father said, "I don't think the city does you much good, Inge."

On Monday, Marilyn called her at the office and asked if she could come over that evening.

"Of course you can," Inge said. And made a note to buy asparagus, which Marilyn loved, a couple of veal cutlets, and fresh lettuce for salad.

"Asparagus," was about all Marilyn said during dinner.

Inge talked about the family, about her mother's joy in the grandchildren, about her father's dwindling practice. Her mother was wondering whether to plant strawberries again. Hard work. Little yield. Marilyn tried to listen but her face had new lines of anguish on it. She played with her napkin as if all of her life was abstract. Her grey dress drooped at the hem. Even her hair looked depressed.

Inge made an effort to cheer her up.

"So my mother's thinking about corn all the time. There's this new strain called Harvest Gold. When she writes 'peaches and cream' on the board by the road-side stand, people drive up wanting dessert and coffee. And get mad when she tells them it's a type of corn. Harvest Gold they should understand."

Marilyn got up from the table and went to where the fireplace would have been if there had been one and sat cross-legged on the rug.

"He said I was different," she said.

Inge had considered this and replied, "He does, at the time, see each one of you as his best, only true love," knowing that it was no comfort.

"He said I should come back to work at Bryden. I could have your job."

"Oh dear."

They sat in silence for a short time and Inge felt that an evil thing, a black vampire or a monstrous turkey vulture had invaded her neat apartment, spoiling it. She thought of how now and then her father had needed exterminators to de-bug his office building and wondered what poison might be needed to get rid of this particular infestation. She made herself, by looking at the photograph of Lake Scugog on the wall, conjure up a peaceful image before she took hold of Marilyn's hand and spoke to her again.

"Go on vacation," she said. "Take a month off. Two weeks even."

"Jim and I are going camping the week after next. We've been planning it for six months. He bought me a Coleman stove for Christmas. He's so excited," Marilyn answered and the tears she had held back came pouring down her face.

Inge put *Sahara* into the VCR and followed it with *The Garden of Allah.*

"She never slept with Boyer."

"But all those others!"

"She was a make-over artist," Marilyn answered.

Inge sat still for a long time after Marilyn had gone. She recalled long sunny afternoons when she and the other kids had played house. She recalled evenings she had spent alone in this very apartment, content with a book and a sandwich, calling home or talking to Marilyn about the last movie. She made plans to take the old farmhouse over some day and make it commercial and live to a background of skirling sandpipers and croaking bullfrogs.

Her mother called and said she couldn't believe how fast the corn was growing this year, forgetting that she had said that last year and the year before and forever. Inge looked again at Lake Scugog, blue that day in sunshine. When she had taken that photograph, the beauty of the landscape had filled her with joy, and she had felt herself to be a fortunate woman: *I have my job and my life. My plans.*

She pictured Marilyn and Jim in their tent in Algonquin Park, making quiet love. And Marilyn there afraid to let go, afraid to let him know her secret. *Don't worry sweetheart*, he would say. *The bears won't get you while I'm here.* Then Marilyn might relax and her cries would blend in with the crickets chirping, the lake lapping on the shore, loons crying. Just like in the movies.

Three days after Marilyn had set off on her trip, Inge asked Janine to field her calls and left the office early. "A dental appointment, Bertrand," she said. He did not care. Nancy the new receptionist had come to give him a message. He was drawing her into his office. He had something to show her.

Next day he put a portfolio down on Inge's desk and stopped to stare.

"Inge!" he said.

"Yes," she replied through newly coloured lips. "You got your mail, didn't you?"

"Sure," he replied and went slowly on his way.

She punched that fragment of conversation into the new file marked *LOVE*, and left it at that. At four she said she had to leave early to go to the beauty salon.

The stylist said her hair was difficult, healthy but difficult, and that a good cut and a light colour would transform her completely.

"Take a good look at yourself in the mirror," he commanded. "You'll never want to go back to this."

She watched the long strands fall and calculated how many months, even years, it would take her hair to grow back to that length. He cut her hair so that it framed her face, covered her high forehead, accentuated her cheekbones. A Scandinavian look that was not surprising given her antecedents.

Next day Bertrand Greene asked her to have a drink after work.

"I'd like you to look at some of these options," he said. "I think we have something to discuss."

The *Love* file grew. It was four pages long by the following Wednesday. He had said variously:

How come I never noticed you were so attractive?

I've been, you know, a little hesitant about asking you out.

You seemed guarded, on a pedestal. I wasn't sure.

I need you, Inge.

I want this to be very special.

You know there have been others but they do not matter, have never mattered.

You are different.

She had said to him:

I didn't think you saw me except as part of the furniture.

Black Ribbon Industries is going to make it by fall.

I love good music too.

I thought you were maybe a little insecure.

A card came from Marilyn. It said sadly, *The weather isn't too good but we're pressing on.*

On the following Tuesday Bertrand came into Inge's office and sat on the edge of her desk like a young lover and handed her a red rose. His wife was out of town. His son away at camp. He wanted to make dinner. Could she? Would she? It would make him so happy.

She looked at his eyes and saw that what she had told Marilyn was true. For the moment, for this day, with her, he was sincere. She had become his best love.

"I'll leave early," she said.

She took great care. The next credit card bill would be huge. It was a necessary investment. She went back to the beauty salon. The cosmetician took her to another room, and she lay under a mask while her fingernails were caressed and polished red. The stylist teased out her hair.

"What colour of outfit are you going to wear?" he asked. And everyone in the salon turned to listen to her answer.

She said, "Well it's a sort of turquoise," and felt them lose faith in her.

On the way to Bertrand's house, she caught sight of herself in a store window and didn't recognise the Inge Johansson who looked back. The image was an alien, a camouflaged being. *This is not me, this is not me*, she murmured aloud as her heels clicked on the sidewalk. And there was the number in brass on the wall of his house. There he was at the doorway of his house, holding the door open for her.

"Love," he said.

He embraced her, made her sit down, gave her wine. He had set out an elegant little feast of deli items. Paté and cheese and French bread and sliced tomatoes. She was used to a more substantial dinner but nibbled delicately at his mouse banquet.

"There have been others. You must know."

"I know," she said. She looked at him from under larger eyelashes pausing for a moment to wonder what they were made of. And then, hoping she wasn't using phrases from his letters, she told him that what mattered was that they were here together, now.

"Love," he said.

In movies, they ripped each other's clothes off and left them where they lay, pants, shirts, socks, underwear, on the stairs, in the hall. In movies, they danced first, and even sang to one another. But he led her upstairs silently and fully clothed not to the marital bed but to the spare room.

They made love and afterwards, as he lay back, smiling and satisfied, and sipped his wine, she told him he was a true earth-mover.

He grew excited and told her his great plan to sell the house; it was a vendor's market, had been since spring. His wife would go back to her home in Quebec. She liked it better there. It was best for her. And then he with Inge could conquer the world. What a team they would make. She was efficient. He had flair. They would be daring about futures, canny about northern mines. Slowly he wound down. His eyes closed.

"I'm going to take a shower," she said.

"Be sure you put towels round the base," he said dozily and closed his eyes again. "It leaks."

His bathroom. His wife's bathroom. Her stuff. His stuff. She found thick towels and put them within reach and turned on the faucet. Inge soaped and sponged her face and body. Lovely warm water washed off her eyelashes, her lipstick, straightened her hair, till she began to feel real again. For ten minutes, fifteen, she let the water stream over her body, making her clean. Restoring her to herself. Restoring Marilyn. She heard happier sighs coming from the North as though Marilyn knew. Marilyn in her tent under the pines could be happy again.

Bertrand the earth-mover was sound asleep. He grunted, breathed heavily. And would not have liked her to see him so old. On his chest the hairs were already grey; his cheeks had sunk in. He sagged. The pill she had slipped into his wine had taken effect.

In movies, at this point, people took lipstick and

wrote cutting remarks on mirrors. Inge put on her clothes and went down to the kitchen and surveyed the knives in their block of wood. She took the carving knife from its slot and ran the blade along her finger. It drew a few drops of blood.

In modern movies, they took knives like that and killed for spite and vengeance.

As she walked back up the stairs carrying the knife, she noticed water dripping through the living room ceiling onto a fine-looking rug patterned in deepest blue and grey and soft pink.

What she was about to do she did for Marilyn, for Janet, for Lucy, for Diane, for Alys, for Rita, for Shauna, for Beth, for Lisa, for the red-haired woman who played the piano, for Greta, for Alex, for Estelle, for Emma, for Joanne, for Sara, for herself. For them all. For all of Bertrand Greene's best loves.

She had watched her father neuter cats and dogs many a time. The trick was to do it with speed and accuracy.

AMONG
THE
HEROES

The hippopotamus wore a yellow bikini over its glossy grey hide and a pair of sunglasses stretched across its broad head. Jenny gave it to me when she left. She was setting out for a new life, lighting out for the Territory, which in this case was Greece. She had met the man at a conference. He was rich and charming and handsome. She went away laughing and dreaming of sun, leaving behind a February city, twenty years of hard work, and me in tears.

I gave her my treasured copy of Euripides to read on the journey.

Her lover took her to Thessaly, and from there I received the first postcard: *Dear Audrey, Retsina, fresh figs, fresh olive oil. No wonder the gods lived here.*

I figured she had no time to read and wouldn't see the passages I'd marked in *Alcestis*, the ones that spoke of friendship and the sacrifices that true friends make for one another.

I had to keep busy. I put the hippo on the bookshelf, repainted the basement apartment, and rented it out to a musician, and after him to a recently divorced bookseller with too many cats.

More postcards came from Jenny. She went to Epidaurus, to Mycenae, to places of ancient life which I would, I thought, have died to see. I began to save, and I put up the rent of the apartment. I had to fumigate it after David moved out and left behind his cats' fleas, sixteen boxes of used paperbacks, and the aura of his frustrated love for me.

My capital dwindled to one thousand three hundred dollars. The smell of thiazane seeped up through the floor. No one wanted to rent the basement. Friends nagged me to sell the house. They made up ads for me, *neat 2bdrm 2storey, granny flat in bsmt,* and told me of neat condos I could get for a song. Useless to tell them I didn't know the words to that tune.

A postcard, picture of the Parthenon. Jenny and her love had moved out to the islands. Friendly Greeks. Ever-flowing wine. She'd seen old marble pillars through a haze of history. Long-unworshipped deities had leered down at her from their pedestals and called her names: *Tourist, alien, dilettante.*

The bank manager offered me a loan against the house. I lowered the rent of the apartment and began to choose what I would wear when I went to meet Jenny in Greece. Simple skirts and shirts, the travel writers said. Garments made of material that can be rolled up without creasing. Painless packing!

People were leaving the city to find cheaper places to live. The bsmt apt stayed vent. If I could bring myself to sell the house, I could afford not only Greece and Italy but Australia and the Outer Hebrides too. But the house had been my parents' place, my only living space ever and, to me, "a neat condo" had the ring of cage bars. Housing prices dropped and lurched. It was a buyer's market.

"Parry Sound."

"Orillia!"

"Not Parry Sound?"

"Orillia, I tell you."

"I could've sworn Parry Sound."

Pinter breakfast talk beside Lake Muskoka. This was my punishment for backing off, for trading in my ticket to Greece and going to spend yet another vacation at my aunt's cottage near Huntsville.

There in the once-wilderness, three cousins, two aunts and one uncle traded family details and told stories that had been funny once. My aunt when she was on her own acted out *Sweet Bird of Youth* with the young man from the gas station, and couldn't wait for her visitors to leave. As for me, mixing the evening drinks, I was the quiet dark one who might make something of herself yet. In the mornings, baking muffins, I was the unclaimed treasure who would make someone a good wife one day. For hours I sat alone on the rocks and wondered why I'd spurned the Isle of Andros for this.

Driving back to town, I could see the city ahead, its tall towers trying to rise above a yellow wreath of pollution. It was time to move into reality, to get a life, to sell the house, to acquire courage, to go to Greece.

And then, one fall day, before I had time to pick out the lucky real estate agent, Jenny returned from her travels, sick to death, weary, pale. Greek doctors had told her there was nothing they could do for her. The rich man had gone on to Rome alone and promised to keep in touch.

She moved back into the basement, and in the evenings, over coffee and brandy, she told me about Greece. She told me about sitting in the ancient amphitheatre, holding my book, weeping to think that long, long ago, men and women in their robes and sandals had sat in that same place listening to the same poetry. And how then, at that moment, the rich man had begun to lose interest in her. Not because she could no longer eat calamari without throwing up, but because she cried at the utter timelessness of things.

"He had no sense of the immortal," she said.

I told her she was better off without him.

After that we said nothing for some time.

The third time she came back from the hospital I gave her the hippo to cheer her up. Set on her bedside table among flowers, it looked all right. She was pleased I'd kept it. She knew it was vulgar, she said. She'd given it to me when she went away to make me understand that I was losing nothing in losing her. It had been that kind of gift.

I was glad I hadn't understood.

She talked again about the play. "It was meant to be funny," she said. The idea that women were so worthless that they should be sacrificed for men. But the audience, still, today, took it seriously.

Her lover hadn't seen the funny side of it either. Even so, I knew she wished that, out of the blue, he would turn up on the doorstep and take her in his arms and weep at his own treachery. I think she spent hours watching for him. And every time the phone rang, she reached for it with fearful eagerness.

Her sickness weighed on my mind. Thoughts of last months, last painful weeks, drove me to despair. In cook books I searched for soothing dishes, superior comfort food. I selected novels to read to her in the time when she became too tired to see the words. I tried to invent little jokes for those final days so that she could once more exit laughing.

Friends of hers and of mine came to talk to her and offer help. "Call us any time," they said, and then ran away to get on with their lives, turning their backs on death.

The doctors at the hospital downtown simply shook their heads. Something caught in such a foreign country! They could do nothing. What could she expect? It was an alien virus. At work I told them I might need time off. I wasn't sure when. Most of the time Jenny looked well, walked well. Only on some days she stayed in bed and stared at the ceiling, her hands plucking at the quilt as though she was rehearsing her last scene.

During the day at work, I saved little incidents to relate to her. But the government trundled on in its boring way and there was little to tell. Secrets didn't filter down to my level and the gossip that raced round the outer offices was trivial unless you knew the players. Which was why, when I thought about it, drama had become my other better life. I hardly ever went to the theatre. Sitting in my chair, a glass of wine beside me, the book in my hand, was enough. No big-headed director was going to intervene between me and the playwright. I didn't need actors to interpret the words for me. The characters moved around me, speaking their lines perfectly.

Jenny laughed at me.

"You have to see the play," she said, "to know what it's really about."

I told her that actors ruin a good play as often as not. I'd read enough reviews to know that.

But she softly replied that my peculiar habit was like staying at home and reading the music instead of going to a concert. I could see nothing wrong with that either.

It was Christmas when I got the first soufflé about right, crisp on top, soft underneath, tempting, tasty. I put the hippo on the table beside the poinsettia and set two places and Jenny crept up the stairs to join me. She made a great effort that day. She didn't flinch when I drank wine while she had juice. She tasted the soufflé and said it was the best thing she'd ever eaten. I told her that Nerisse at the office had told everyone that the head of Accounting was having an affair with Gloria in Archives and it turned out to be untrue but he began to behave so strangely that his wife became suspicious and came to the office one day and made a scene. I kept on talking because I couldn't bring myself to ask Jenny to wear a paper hat and listen to joyful carols. We spent the evening watching *It's a Wonderful Life*.

Her mother called again from Florida and said she had just had another hip replacement and would be up to visit soon when the weather got warmer, and she could move easily, in spring, late spring. Jenny apologised for not being there to help her, and said she was feeling much, much better. Sarah Bernhardt would've been proud of the strength in her voice.

On the second of March, a day when winter had decided to take another swingeing blow at the city, the phone rang and it was Helga. I hadn't seen her for years.

"I've got two days," she said. "I can come and stay? We'll have great times. We'll have dinner out. Don't do a thing. Just give me a bed."

Enter Helga. She came in looking like an Amazon. She was the picture of health and delight as she strode into my house to alter lives and claim what had been promised. The space appeared to shrink.

I showed her to the spare room I'd cleaned up for when Jenny had to move upstairs. Helga admired the old photos and ornaments left over from the family life that had existed here once. Even the glass bowl of pot-pourri, mother's own make, was standing on the little dresser where it had always stood. Helga kissed me and told me I hadn't changed and said she'd be down in a few minutes.

She found me in the kitchen mixing a yogurt and fruit drink for Jenny. We talked cheerfully of her journey from Ottawa and her forthcoming job. She teased me about being a stick-in-the-mud, same old office, same old house, same old Audrey. She poured wine for us both and drank hers quickly and poured another and told me a funny story about a man she'd met on the plane. Everything was fine till she said, "And what weirdo have you got living in the basement now?"

And then I couldn't stop the tears. Snivelling, I told her about Jenny, about the hard work, the strain, the awfulness of living with someone who was simply accepting mortality.

Helga shrieked at me, "You idiot! You could've said no. You didn't have to do this. I have other friends. What do you think I am? And what about her mother! And how did she get so sick?"

It was at Pompeii as far as Jenny knew. A very hot

day. She had looked closely at the mosaic and the stark shadows of men and women incinerated in the midst of life. She and he had walked along the street and then, on an impulse, he wanted to see Carthage. There was a quick change of plans. Feeling overtired, Jenny had gone with him to Tunis and a few days later was caught with a shivery fever. *A kind of malaria*, they told her. *Go home*, they told her. And she had realised she had no home but mine.

"You should've told me," Helga said. "You should've put me off. I could have stayed with Brian and Mary. You let me drink and make jokes. How could you?"

Of all the people I admire, Helga tops the list. She goes around the world, caring nothing for her own comfort, remaining strong through jungle and desert. She has set up posts for volunteers to help out with famine and with disease and tried against great odds to make the world a better place.

She looked at me then, her skin battered by sun, her eyes glaring out of that dark face, accusing me of being insensitive.

"You're my friend," I said.

"This is too much," she replied.

"I was supposed to lie to you?"

In ancient Greece, among the heroes, friendship was paramount, hospitality a moral law. Admetus hid his family tragedy and said, "Welcome friend, come right in," and told his guests to make free of the house.

I could see nothing wrong with that.

"I'll go see her," Helga said.

"Let me see how she is first."

Later on, I'd been warned, Jenny would become fractious and blame all those who had been good to her, turn on her friends as death reached out to take hold of her. But for the moment, she was all gratitude and love. And of course she would be delighted to see Helga.

I left them together. Their relationship at school had been one of rivalry. And at first I sensed Helga's feeling that Jenny was trying to upstage her one last time. Jenny had become the drama and all of us were tiptoeing round the edge, minor characters, while she took centre stage, she and her invisible co-star.

Helga was heroic. She called APSO and told them she was taking all the leave due to her. She stayed on and when I was at work took trays to Jenny, sat with her, giving her comfort with the skill learned among strangers. One day, when I came back at six, I found she'd moved Jenny's bed single-handedly into my dining room so that Jenny could look out of the window. She'd arranged for a nurse to come every day to bathe and feed the patient.

Then a new tenant moved into the basement apartment, a quiet, non-rent-paying occupant who wouldn't leave till he got what he wanted. He was always there beneath us, waiting till we had our backs turned, waiting to creep up the stairs and seize his prey, giving no notice of the hour and time when he would pounce.

But as long as Helga was there, strong and defiant, he wouldn't dare to make his move. I left her with confidence. She made coffee for visitors, for friends who, sensing that the denouement was close, stopped in now and then to hold Jenny's hand.

In late April, Jenny's mother decided she was well enough to make the journey. She couldn't drive but would leave the car in Fort Lauderdale and fly back to see her daughter. Jenny smiled after she had talked to her on the phone. Smiled and lay back exhausted.

On my birthday, Nerisse brought cake and wine to the office, and we drank to the uncertain future of our department. We laughed and talked about Marlene Dietrich who had just died. In a husky voice, Robin sang, "'Johnny, when it's your birthday, I'll spend the night with you.'" And after that, much later than usual, I went home, light-headed, humming a love song.

I stopped to look at the buds on the maple tree, the delphinium shoots. A stranger pushed past me as I walked up the path. One of Helga's friends? A new nurse? I turned but the figure had blended into the landscape and disappeared.

The door was open, not locked. I ran inside calling out, "Here's the birthday girl!"

Jenny's body was covered with a sheet.

"Just a moment ago," Helga said.

She was arranging flowers on the table. In fury, I rushed to where she was standing. My hands clawed at her throat and I was shouting, "You were here to save her. You came to stay. I made you welcome. You were supposed to bring her back to life."

Helga pushed me away. I staggered and fell.

"Who do you think I am?" she said and ran out of the room crying. From the kitchen she called out again, "Who do you think I am!"

On the floor, with Jenny's limp body only a few feet away, I sat and howled for my friend. No one was going to lead a veiled figure back to me and say, *Welcome this woman to your house.* It wasn't that play. It would not end in cries of joy.

I picked up the china hippo and threw it against the

wall. It broke into so many fragments that not even Zeus could have put it back together.

"I'm sorry. I was out of my mind," I said to Helga.

"I would have done it if I could," she answered. And for a moment she did look noble, all-powerful, able, like Herakles, to bring the dead back to life.

"None of us can do that, Audrey," she said. "It was never true, you know. Just a story."

I wanted to hit her again. Stories! Truth! Who dares to say which is which. Who knows if he can beat down death or not till he tries.

I called her mother and she said, through dreadful tears, "She died in good company. A legend died today." We put off the funeral till she arrived. A closed coffin. A cremation. Her mother had known her vigorous and well.

When she was packing up to go to Somalia, Helga said, "Just before she died, Jenny was talking about that play she saw in Greece. She wanted to know if they lived happily ever after. I didn't know what she was talking about."

I knew. And I knew that no woman could respect a man after he had been prepared to let her die in his place. How could she? But I would have said, *Sure Jenny, Alcestis forgave him and they were happy all the rest of their days.*

Two weeks later, a letter arrived from the rich man. He hoped Jenny felt better, begged her to return to him; he missed her, he was miserable, he knew that she was his only love. I sealed it up again and wrote, in her handwriting, "Returned Unopened" on the envelope and mailed it back to him.

It was the last thing I could do for her. In the name of friendship.

BRIDE
OF
THE
SEA

They stood in Venice, not on the Bridge of Sighs but a little farther away, on the bank of a small, murky canal. Where was there, after all, to stand in Venice but on the banks of canals or on bridges peering down? No one had invited them to a Ca'd'Oro or a Ca'da Mosca to stand on a balcony, and none of it had been as romantic as they had hoped. And now they were staring into the dark water wondering whether the effluent from their washbasin in the small hotel poured into the canal at this point.

She wanted to make something fine of the moment. He wished they were still in Belgium.

"I am married to the sea, married to the sea," she murmured.

He gripped her hand, not pleasantly. He had liked Belgium best. Belgians were real. A Belgian plumber would not have dared to kiss the hand of his employer. Belgian plumbers were dour men in berets who did not smile and who spoke a language even she could not understand.

It had taken him three weeks of searching to find those earrings. He had muttered and stammered ridiculous replies when store clerks had asked him if his wife was slim, if she wore make-up, if her face was round or square, and if he would like to see their more expensive lines. But that was in Toronto where the streets were paved and people understood him when he spoke.

"Darryl," she said. And for the first time in his life, he wanted to change his name. "They trod here. Their footsteps are here."

History thrilled her. She was standing where doge after doge had walked. Richly dressed retinues had passed by here on their way to welcome the Pope or to see someone tortured. When he had not responded to her cries of delight, her recognition of works of art, or to the gobbets of history she read aloud to him from the guide book, she had, finally, called him a dismal pig. Their day had been like that, even before the disaster.

He did want to be happy. He wanted her to teach him how to achieve a state of pleasure in his surroundings. He had relied on her to make him happy. And following her, listening as she threw those long names around, Contarini, Malipiero, as though these people were her personal friends, he understood that she lived in another world which she carried everywhere with her and which was still closed to him.

"Tell me what's wrong," she had insisted when they got back to their room earlier, in the afternoon. "I'm not going one more step till you tell me why you're so miserable."

What could he say? Could he say that she had something he could not attain? Could he say he was jealous? Could he say that he longed to throw the guide book into the Grand Canal? That he liked best their regular life where both of them went out to work and came home in the evening and sat together, pleasantly watching TV? Could he cry out that she was foreign to him in this alien place?

He said the only thing that was left for him to say, "I don't like that outfit you're wearing."

In amazement, she had put her hands to her head, and that was when she had noticed the earring was missing. There had been two. Now there was only one. Where had it gone! She had washed. She had changed. She had been wearing it when they returned to the hotel. He had noticed it glinting in the light.

They scurried about the room then like rats, grubbing round on the floor, rushing their hands over surfaces, their fingers up and down the drapes, shifting the bed to scrabble beneath.

"I took them off to wash," she said.

"It must be in the U-bend," he had shrieked, truly shrieked, surprising himself by his own loudness and by the fact that he had been able to stop himself from crying out the price in dollars and then in lire.

"I thought I'd put them both back on."

She is the only woman I know who doesn't have pierced ears, he had told his mother, thinking it to be an advantage at the time.

The phrase book was little help. It uselessly explained how to ask the way to museum and how to let a stranger know that you were free on Wednesdays. But there was no neat sentence which said, in Italian,

Please, I need a plumber, my earring has gone down the drain.

Down in the dim hallway of the Casa San Aurelio, he had stood behind her, hopping from one leg to the other while she slowly and with selfish delight had found words to explain their dilemma to the man at the desk.

"Non domani. At once. Subito! Capisce?"

And they had returned to the room to await the arrival of their saviour.

The plumber was a cheerful dark-haired man with a cap and scarf that proclaimed him to be a supporter of Juventus. He spoke some English. Downstairs he had turned the water off. Cries from the hallway had made it clear that he had turned off all the water in the little building. Showing him the remaining earring, she had communicated the problem to him. Then he had taken out the piece of pipe from under the sink and with a thin wire poked gently, gently, through the straight pipe that led down into the unknown. He probed and twisted and then withdrew the wire.

He sat back on his heels and smiled. "In the canal. Possibile. Eh. Spozalizio del mar. Now she is married to the sea."

Married to the sea! Of course she had read about that. Darryl knew she would have read about that. She was in ecstasy over it. A ceremony going back donkey's years. She was in their ancient world, in a boat going about beyond the Lido, throwing gold ring after gold ring into the sea. The gold rings of centuries. Annually a ring was cast away. From the plumber she was learn-ing superlatives. Mirabilissime! And giving no thought to the gold and diamond bauble which had cost him much time and nine hundred and fifty dollars. There was, though, no point in thinking of earrings separately. She was not the sort of woman who would wear only one, rakishly in one ear.

She went on talking now to this plumber in two broken languages, churning up more history, enjoying even this particular moment.

"And there was great feast."

"Mirabile."

"The signora has no need of jewels."

Darryl had heard of people chewing carpet in a rage and wished that the brown rug on the floor looked more appetising.

"Might as well throw the other down after it," she was saying, grinning at this stranger in his multicoloured cap.

"No. No," Darryl yelled, snatching it from her, putting it safely in his pocket.

"My husband is material," she said to the plumber.

The plumber, il trombaio, looked Darryl up and down and smirked. "Che peccato," he had replied.

He had kissed her hand, screwed the pipe back together and gone, cheerfully, to turn the water back on.

Darryl had wanted time to mourn the earring. It was something good, lost. But she came from a light-hearted family. His mother had said at the wedding reception that they were a people who looked on the bright side and that no good would, eventually, come of it. But he at that time had hoped their outlook was infectious. *Her work is difficult*, he had told his mother then and had received the expected answer, *Did we call you Darryl for nothing?*

And then, in that narrow room in a little Italian

hotel, he was filled with misery because he could not reach into her soul and she had lost his gift.

"We're both hungry," Andrea said to forestall his anger.

"I am not hungry," he had replied.

"You've sulked all day because you didn't like what I was wearing. And now you'll sulk over an earring. I'm sorry about the earring. I'm really sorry, Darryl. I loved these earrings. They were the nicest gift I ever had. I feel sad about it. But we can't let it spoil these few days. This is VENICE!"

He thought of Germany. Its massive castles had in some way suppressed her. But even there, men in beer gardens had cast their eyes on her, sensing her capacity for joy, raising large mugs and shouting "Prosit!"

As for these Italians, their frivolous nature was apparent everywhere. It was well-known that they were a childish people. Well-known to him at least. Why else these lions with wings, these masks to hide their faces, masks with feathers and sparkling decoration, painted purple and pink and yellow?

She had put on a skirt with a floral pattern on a blue background and a jacket of the same blue but without the flowers. Round her neck she was wearing a gold chain that someone else had given her. Her wedding ring, still on her finger at least, glowed.

So after the plumber had left, and after Darryl had shouted out the true price after all, they had gone out to eat. He had gone with her. What else was there for him to do but go, or stay in this dimly lit room alone.

He had watched her eat a dish of baked fish followed by figs and cream, and now he was standing beside her on the bank of this minor canal wishing himself back in his office where the computer knew his name and the Fax machine fed him daily evidence of his place in the world.

"There's no use," she said, "looking at the water like this. If it's down there, and it isn't, we can't dive in after it. I've said I'm sorry. I'm tired of trying to make you have a good time. And if you're going to stay in this dark mood, I'm going to see Venice by myself."

A gondolier, who looked very like the plumber, called out to them to come and ride in his gondola.

"Si, si," she responded. "Quanto costa?"

And quickly, without waiting for a reply, she hopped into the boat and the gondolier pushed off onto the water and Darryl was left standing there, alone, a man on his own, speechless, with one gold earring in his pocket.

She sailed away from him, standing up, waving, shouting, "I am married to the sea! Married to the sea," and left him there, like a fool, with one earring and no wife. And besides, "You've got the plane tickets," he shouted after her. "You've got everything."

He climbed into the next gondola and set off to follow, saying to the gondolier one of the two forceful Italian words he knew, "Andiamo!"

He called to her, "I don't care about the money. You are married to me. To me."

But the gondolier, hoping for a large tip, was singing loudly, and Darryl's words floated on the water, like the scraps of paper which came floating towards him and which looked very like his return ticket to Canada and little pieces of a marriage certificate. Leaning down he thought he could read the date on a fragment as it floated by, May the 6th, 1992.

The gondolier, conscientious, stopped singing to point out San Giorgio, various palaces, strange dark places, buildings that rose out of the water like louring monsters, sinister, with water lapping at the walls, encouraging rats. Darryl would have preferred to see it all in ignorance and endow the places with his own idea of history.

"We pass now the Palazzo where, if you will believe, a doge was murdered because he had too much taken. Many times our treasure was stolen by others. Napoleone when he came took everything. Our lions, and before that in the fire of 1577, also we lost paintings and if you look now to the left . . ."

Darryl hurled his other imperative at the gondolier, "Taci!" And the man was silent.

She had long been out of sight.

Silently the darkening buildings passed them by. Other gondolas carrying parties of cheerful tourists or languid couples overtook them. Darryl sat bolt upright, counting the cost.

After the ride, he ate a whole pizza and then went back to the room which after all was paid for. In her guidebook, he read that the ring in those first days had been thrown into the water as an act of propitiation to certain gods. Only later had the story about marriage grown up around the ceremony. She was involved in a myth.

He lay down on the bed and slept a sad sleep.

She was there beside him next morning. He woke knowing that there would be coffee and bread for breakfast. The air in the city had changed. That strange heaviness which oversets Venice and had in earlier times caused people to get sick and die had dissipated in a light breeze. Now it was the pleasant place, the glorious place it was meant to be. The sunlight on the walls of the old church out there in the square turned it into a sanctuary.

He was reassured. He knew that the earring was a sacrifice that had to be made. A gift to the gods of the place to secure future well-being. He had given it to her, for her to do with as she wished. If she carelessly let it fall into the sewer system, did it matter?

All the same, his morning smile was forced.

Silently, she got dressed. He smiled again. He smiled twice more.

She produced the ticket; she produced, like a rabbit from a hat, the marriage certificate and set them both down in front of him. And a bright object flew out of her purse onto the rug. He knelt down. There was the earring, the lost one. The other, its mate, was still in his pocket. Crouching, he held them both in the palm of his hand. And from that position, he looked up, looked at her calves in their pale skins, her skirt, the one he had said yesterday he did not like, the blouse, the neck with its gold chain, the face, the look of reproachful compassion in her eyes.

"Let's go to Torcello," he said.

"And Burano?"

"Where you like."

She scooped the earrings from his hand.

"Are you," he said, and his life hung on the question, "still married to the sea?"

"The sea is fickle," she replied, and stroked his hair.

He knew that for all his life he would never lose the image of her smile at that moment and would spend a lifetime trying to fathom the mystery of it.

THE
THIRD
WISH

It was cold for May in Los Angeles. Norah had on her
moccasins. These last years, they'd been the best of
things for her bony feet, awry as they were with arthritis. She'd put on her navy blue dress with the white
jacket and was waiting by the door when Charlie drove
up. As they rolled along through the palm-lined streets,
she looked at his fine profile. He'd been such a pretty
child that people would stop to ask if he was not the
child of this famous actor or that, thinking her to be
his nurse.

"Drop me off here, please," she said at the corner
of the crescent. "I'll not be long."

"If you're sure, Mother."

"I'm sure, dear."

Norah got out of the car and walked slowly towards
the house, holding on to the red rose she'd bought fresh
that morning. And there she was, the house herself,
stone and solid and splendid still. The trees had grown
tall to shade the front. The main door was painted
white, and Norah had no doubt that the furniture in-

side was as grand as Madame's had ever been. The people in there, may their lives be a joy to them, were surely as fine as the chairs themselves. She wanted to knock on the door, knowing that she never in this world would, and tell them that she had lived there once. Once upon a time she, Norah O'Donnell, had owned this house.

Perhaps the door would open and a kindly person invite her in, offer her tea, listen to her memories. She could hear Madame's voice, clear as it was always in her mind, singing, *What am I bid for my apple?*

Norah sat down on the low wall and was lost to time, fifty-three years lost.

An apple they say keeps the doctor away. Madame's song drew her back to those past days. It was before the war and the young Norah lifted her hands from the harsh water and sighed for Ireland. Her only desire being that Madame would remember to pay her. For wasn't Joe out waiting on another gold-paved street, part of the long line that snaked round corners far out of sight of success. The rent was due in two days and not enough money in her purse to buy them a decent dinner.

The floor tiles were the best Italian, and she herself would never have chosen them. Dirt showed in the pattern of leaves, and dust got into the cracks. Plain linoleum would have been easier to clean. Just a wipe with a damp cloth, and a good scrub once a week.

"Norah!"

Madame was by now in the kitchen. She stood there, wearing her old trousers and a shirt much too large and held out her hand for the brush. With her other hand she set down ten dollars on the table.

Norah got up and poured out the dirty water from the pail, ran clean water into it, and added the scented soap Madame preferred. She stirred it with a wooden spoon and set the bucket down beside Madame who was already on her knees. And Madame looked up at her and in her husky voice said, "Danke."

She always spoke German after she had made love. Her lover standing in the doorway with his camera, commanded, "Turn your head a little to the left. Now smile."

And after a moment he went away to get dressed. A short fellow he was, but Joe had said that little men were often well-endowed. Though Norah found it hard to imagine their love-making. Madame with the little film-maker. Two growling animals scrabbling at each other in a foreign language.

Madame said in an interview, "He makes me what I am. I hurry each day to view the rushes to see what he has made of me. I am his creature." And Norah, reading the magazine, thought, *For shame to be anyone's creature.*

Even scrubbing a floor Madame was a picture, as if he had managed to arrange the light and the set just so to her best advantage. Her golden hair shone and her slim body moved snake-like as she twisted and turned. She began to hum as she worked, the one about the blond baby, one of her gentle songs. It had seemed to Norah to be a poor sort of song to sing to an infant till Madame had sung the words to her in English and waltzed her round the room as she sang. *Blond hair and dark blue eyes, my baby.* Like your eyes, Norah.

Joe said Madame was a poor actress and couldn't really hold a tune. What would she have made of

"Danny Boy," a true test for a singer? But he had never heard her at home in the mornings with an audience of one, never seen her close up.

Norah wiped her hands and took off her apron. She had already done the other rooms except for the bedroom but couldn't leave till she'd cleared away in the kitchen.

Looking to make sure the little film-maker was upstairs, she went into the drawing room and sat down. She had never sat in their fine padded chairs before, only rubbed the wooden frames with oil and used a stiff brush on the upholstery. She leaned against the blue velvet and conjured her family, Ma and Dad and Sonny and Maureen, out of the air. They thought her to live like this. A woman of leisure being brought good bits of food on trays. A chicken leg, fat and juicy. Soda bread warm from the oven, slathered with butter and jam.

My teeth weren't good enough for films, she wrote to them at home, *but I have work and will send money soon.* And she added, *I miss your songs, Dad.* For he sang lyrics with real sweet sadness in them like "Kitty of Coleraine" and "The Star of the County Down."

If I had a house like this, Norah thought, as she sat there in the soft chair, I would get rid of the Chinese panels and the woolly rug that holds every bit of grime. I would paper the walls first with creamy paper, a small rose pattern. I would bring in linen from Ireland and dressers from Wales and chairs from Italy and a carpet from Persia.

She closed her eyes from weariness and wished very hard that someone would bring her a cup of coffee and a cigarette. And exactly then, right at that moment, the little film-maker himself came into the room carrying two cups.

She leapt up, almost crashing into him, eager to get out of the way.

"Sit down," he ordered. He knew nothing of gentle requests.

And he put one of the cups of coffee into her hand and then offered her a cigarette. Courteously, he bent forward to light it for her. He put the gold lighter back in his pocket and rested his hand on her knee. And she imagined him green, a little green man with a pointed hat, capable of magic.

"Tell me how you live."

Startled, she spilt some of the coffee on her skirt but then understood that it was research for a picture so to please him she recited a life: Joe constantly looking for better work, awful-looking beetles in the kitchen, noise in the streets, water dripping down on wet days from the ceiling, vicious people in the halls at night.

She was close to tears herself with the misery of it all, and the man was looking at her as if through a lens, close up.

Norah sipped the coffee in a leisurely way and tried to listen as the man explained his idea to her. *I could live like this*, she thought. And he was saying, "It's a great theme, you see, a story of people and the business of survival."

Madame, wiping her hands on a towel, came into the room, thin eyebrows raised in surprise.

Norah stood up and got away and went off to empty the bucket, to clean in the corners that Madame had missed. One day Madame had caught her at it, doing the corners, mopping up the little leftover dribs of water, and had yelled at her. And she had said in reply, because she was tired and didn't care that day if she kept the job or not, "I can't sing. You can't clean floors."

Later Madame had given her a lace handkerchief, and Norah had taken it home and put it away in her box, a biscuit tin with a picture of the Mountains of Mourne on the lid.

So on this morning when Norah had her coat on, what did Madame do but come into the kitchen carrying a silky blue and white scarf.

"I want you to have this," she said.

"Oh Madame, I couldn't."

"Come on, Norah, to please me."

She came close and wound the scarf round Norah's neck and kissed her on both cheeks.

"See how the blue matches your fine Irish eyes. Those träuen blauen Augen."

In those days the house was painted green. The door which she wiped often, which she opened for people whose teeth and hair and jewels shone and who were called stars, was a pale grey colour. Their faces and words were like a puzzle now, in pieces, needing to be put together to make sense.

Norah, Liebling, he wants to talk to you.

Sit down Norah and tell me how the people talk to each other.

Can you work an extra night, dear Norah?

Any luck today, Joe?

I came close, darling. Very close.

Norah, I want you to have this.

Madame you're too generous.

One day it was the white impractical coat. Norah, living not on strawberries and caviar but on sandwiches and spaghetti, could barely fasten it but wore it all the same. Joe was disturbed by this kind of generosity but she explained Madame's way of giving, how it was she loved to share her wealth because weren't some people guilty about having so much and didn't it ease her conscience.

The postcards from Ireland made her cry, although the pictures on them, white cottages and green lanes, were nothing like the stone terrace where they had lived in Belfast, sharing their lives with a number of neighbours.

The movie was begun. Actors were playing their parts. And the little film-maker took her to the set one day, and she watched him stamping around the building that was to be their apartment, made of board and paper with a wall or two missing. She tried to tell him about the colour, but he wasn't the kind of man to listen to anyone else. He had a temper like a wee jackal.

She was out at the back of the house putting out the rubbish, and Madame was inside singing, trying on clothes. He came through the house shouting, shouting as if through his megaphone, "You are not mysterious." It seemed to be his last word.

A new lover, an actor this time, moved in and then moved out. And after that, one more handsome than the others asked Madame to move in with him, into his house further up the canyon. She was slow making up her mind.

Norah, dusting the table, found an opened bottle of wine and took a glass of it and sat down again in the blue chair, looking out of the window, rehearsing her own part in a movie no one would ever make. She was wearing a fine long gown, welcoming her guests, grandly assigning places to them, offering them caviar and toast and champagne. And her Dad was sitting in a chair of honour, nodding to one and all, proud as could be, brought over first class on the *Queen Mary* by her and Joe who was now rich as the Emperor of Abyssinia from starring in his first movie.

Outside, it was dull, one of those July days when a haze settled over the place and it was too hot to breathe.

Leaning back in that fine upholstered chair, Norah wished with all her might that all the coolness in the house was hers. The apartment was too hot to sleep in. Too hot for living. The night around them was alive with the sound of quarrelling.

"You look as if you belong there, Norah," Madame said, coming close to her, sitting opposite.

"Ah but I don't," Norah replied but didn't get up for her feet were like two boiled lobsters and she didn't ever want to put her shoes on again. "I don't belong here."

"Why not?" Madame said. Just that. Why not!

Joe shouted out. He leapt about. Pranced a kind of jig round her when she showed him the key. *Gave you the house! A house! Paid for. Oh Norah. My love. My love. Now we shall be well. Now we shall be fine. We shall be all manner of things well.*

And Norah joined in his jig for a while, wondering though how they would effect the move and how they would live in so much space and who would dig the garden. And Joe sang "'I've got me a comfortable wife and house / To rid me of the devil in my shoes.'"

Her Dad had never trusted him.

Their friends in the apartment building gave them a party and helped shift the furniture out to the lorry Joe had borrowed from a man he'd met in the studio queues. There were tears. They had all been like one family, sharing what they had, suffering together, happy together. And now Norah's good fortune put a distance between them. Joe said, "We'll have parties. You'll be the first." And Stan from across the way presented them with a housewarming gift of towels that were soft and green for Ireland. Norah held one of the towels to her face and cried into it.

This house was mine, she said to the wall, to the white front door. The sitting room, which had looked so luxurious with Madame's furniture, became poor with their two worn chairs and oak table where the grand piano had been. It lacked the fine flower arrangements. The figures in the Chinese wallpaper seemed to be mocking her and Joe. In the bedroom, their bed looked small. The wool cover, a wedding gift, was nothing in comparison to the zebra-skin spread that had been there before. And there was no huge mirror where they might, had Joe not been so shy and always wanted the light off, have watched themselves make love.

But she'd walked through the house aware of ownership, seeing it fine again, imagining Joe working, moving up, his face on billboards.

Joe said, "This is but the beginning. You'll see. When luck changes, it stays changed. "'I'll grow respected at my ease.'"

Madame moved into the actor's house, and Norah went there every day except Sunday and cleaned and scrubbed as before. The actor was a dream, charming and slow-speaking. In bed at nights, Norah wondered what he was like as a lover and imagined him wonderful. Some days the rooms all smelt of sex, and Norah on her knees or reaching up to clean the corners could feel it about her, disturbing, making her restless. She sat in the fine chair in the larger living room with a glass of their whisky and wished the actor would come in and take her right there on the thick white rug and make love to her and kiss her with his fine lips. And whisper to her that Madame need never know. Need never know, he kept murmuring, stroking her 'lovely black hair.'

The film-maker was a chance visitor to Madame's new mansion, surly because his movie had been stopped by the studios. There was war in Europe and they wanted heroic tales. He wanted to go to Paris and couldn't because the Germans had occupied it. He seemed to blame Madame. And Madame, to aggravate him, sang her songs in German and Norah was glad some evenings to get home.

Madame was a picture in uniform. She came into the kitchen and said, "I'm going for a soldier." It was

her foreignness that made her words sometimes pro-
phetic.,

On a December evening as warm as summer, Joe
said, "We'll have a tree, a big tree. And a party." By
then they had four chairs. Two of them Joe had found
in the rich people's garbage and painted. All the rent
money now went on keeping up the house, on clothes
for him so that he should look like a man who owned a
house and not like the husband of a woman who went
out to clean. The house had him in its grip. He went
off to line up more confident than before, sure that
each day was to be the lucky one.

In distant Europe, war started. And Joe did go, in
an honest way, to the recruiting office, but they turned
him down on account of his eyes, and there was a little triumph on his face when he reported this to Norah.
There. I told you I wasn't fit for heavy work. She
showed him the electricity bill, and he said it was her
house and she should ask Madame for money to keep
it up.

All the well-known people came to Madame's party
that Christmas Eve. Norah in the kitchen, trying to
keep up with the dishes, with the caterers, hoped she
would have a chance to take some of the food home.
The money she had set aside for heat and light left
scarcely enough for a pound of sausage for their dinner tomorrow let alone a fat chicken. She tried though
to laugh as the others did, helping herself to a little
something when she had time, thinking how comfortable it would be to go home to the three rooms in the
apartment building, to their old friends.

The glittering people, laughing and carefree, went
into the dining room to eat turkey and ham and fig pie

and salad. Madame came into the kitchen and kissed her on both cheeks and called her a treasure and told her to go home to spend Christmas in her house and gave her a gift wrapped in silver paper and threw the red gown over her arm.

"You've given me so much," Norah said.

"Don't be silly," Madame replied, looking at her for a moment as though she would change places with her to be the receiver instead of the giver. And it was a gift of a look which Norah didn't know how to accept.

"You have beautiful hair, Norah. So dark. So thick."

"No woman," Joe said, snatching the bracelet in its shiny box from her, "would give such a gift to a woman unless she had done something unspeakable. It's known the kind of woman she is. So that's why she gave you a house."

And then Norah shrieked out those words about work and idleness and why had she ever left Ireland for this. A passer-by had sent for the cops, and Joe had hit her, just the once, and then turned on the first policeman who came in the door.

Joe's gift to her was on the bed. A box with a card on it, *Merry Christmas, Norah, something for your tired feet*. A pair of fine slippers made of deerskin with a fringe round the top.

She took two aspirins and locked the door for the night and knew without looking that the money in the jar on the kitchen shelf was all gone. She wept. And slept a little and gave way to the sin of despair. The light of Christmas morning shining on the bedroom walls brought her round again. Did she not have a little power? She could wish! She could wish for the world. Had not her previous three wishes been granted?

The day after, she crept into the actor's house. The guests were gone. He and Madame were asleep upstairs. In the dining room, in the kitchen, there were plates and glasses, and food on the floor and all of it left for her to clear away.

Before she put on her apron, Norah sat down in the drawing room, in the blue chair, and closed her eyes and wished as hard as she could for five hundred dollars to pay the bills and buy curtains for the house and pay the fifty dollars the court would demand to set Joe free.

Charlie would be getting tired waiting. In no time it would be a regular hot Los Angeles day. Norah nodded towards the East where every morning the sun rose regardless of whether she could see it or not. And to where she knew Europe lay.

Madame had died over there. A recluse these past twenty years, they said. With someone like herself to look after her, perhaps another Norah to whom she gave rich gifts.

She set the single rose down in front of the path and walked back to the car. She'd known for a long time that the wish she made that Boxing Day morning in the actor's house had been a wish too many. Her fourth wish. Everybody knew that the limit for wishes was three. Christmas over, strangers came to call her to account for unpaid bills. And the move back to the old apartment had been an injury to her pride.

Charlie could never understand why she stayed in the old building though he had many a time offered her a better place.

"All right, Mother?"

"Fine, Charlie."

"I'll buy you lunch."

"If you have time."

"I'm not due at the studio till six."

It was again the anniversary of the end of the war in Europe. Where Joe too lay. After his night in jail he had weaseled his way into the army and gone to Africa and Italy, and no amount of sitting in any kind of chair and wishing with all her soul had brought him back to her. She had lost the chance to live with him into old age till his poetry wore grooves in her mind and till he too had to cushion his feet against hard stones.

Charlie would take her to a fancy place for lunch where he was known, not minding her moccasins, her wispy hair.

As they drove he sang to her in that clear voice inherited from his grandfather, "'If you ever go across the sea to Ireland.'"

She listened and didn't speak, and when they stopped at the traffic lights, he leaned over and kissed her and said, "She was a remarkable woman."

"Generous to a fault," Norah answered, touching his face. Quietly she gave thanks to whom-it-may-concern for granting her third wish in such a truly fine way.

TIME
TRAVEL

"Marlene Dietrich is dead, Mrs. P."

Amber Papadakis could hear their voices but she didn't reply. She very rarely spoke to them. They reared up in front of her unsummoned, ghostly white and blue shapes offering her pills and food. All of them smelled of disinfectant, and none of them ever had one useful thing to say.

They said Marlene was dead but the world hadn't come to an end. Music continued. The train from Leeds to Skipton ran as usual past the ruins of Kirkstall Abbey, its stone window-frame seeming, on this summer day, to dangle unattached over the trees. The child with the impish face and flip-brim hat watched sixteen elderly hikers with backpacks and solid boots get off the train at Keighley. Not one of them was younger than the grandmother who pulled the girl onto her knee as the train set off again.

Amber caught sight of her own time-stained face reflected in the window and turned away, envying the child's unspoilt complexion, envying the grandmother.

Envying the hikers as the train left them behind and cut its way through the moors. Sharp Haw, Rough Haw, Pin Haw, were coming into view. Beacon hills in ancient times when Roman legions in clanking armour beat pathways into the grass. To the beat of a drum.

Amber travelled this route often and knew the way by heart.

She chose to follow the hikers as they took the bus to Haworth. *Look at that windmill*, one of them said. *Grotesque*, another replied. They climbed the path past the old churchyard with its ghostly stones and disturbed a man in his allotment nursing a pet goat. Amber let them stride on over rocks and heath towards Top Withens without her. *These are my roots*, she said, pulling up a clump of heather and shaking the soil off it.

She was back on the train, rubbing her feet on the floor.

It was cold outside. Somebody said, "Well this is Canada. This is Toronto." She stamped snow off her boots as she came into the studio. The producer said to the actors, "All right, everybody, I want you to move your feet as you talk." The sound technician had cut up a glossy magazine and strewn the shreds on the floor round the microphone. She and two others shuffled as they read their lines. It was a trick to make listeners think they were hiking over tough, shiny moorland grass. That play had something to do with seagulls and a cruel father and none of them had liked it but they'd done their best and it had gone on to win a prize. A prize that might have been a silver cup or an ivory seagull.

"What's wrong, Amber?" somebody asked but she

paid no attention. (She had come across the sleeping youth hereabouts and was looking for his tracks.)

They told her Marlene Dietrich had died and right away she heard her sister singing. She joined in. A child wearing a paper horn leapt across the stage shouting "I'm a unicorn," wanting recognition.

"Yes," she said to the interviewer who sat beside her, holding her wrist, "I traipsed over here to this country with my love and my sewing machine and my ignorance. My heart wrapped up in a silk handkerchief. Expecting love to last forever. I was a child prodigy you know. I was encouraged at home. There was no television then."

The drawing room walls were covered in pale yellow flowered paper. A frieze round the top was decorated with brown and orange leaves which became faces if you stared at them too long. A couch and large chair covered in matching brown and grey velvet filled half the room. Who had embroidered the screen near the fireplace? An old woman who had gone blind patted Amber's head. The three-tier wooden cakestand held a lemon sponge cake, tea biscuits, tiny sandwiches. Mary Foster came to the end of "I Hear a Brown Bird Singing," and Arthur from next door was waiting to be asked to bellow out "Drake's Drum" in sinister bass tones.

The soldier from Canada, still in uniform, limping now, leaned down and said, "But this little one sings." His voice was kind as he pushed her forward. She nodded to her mother at the piano as she had been taught, preparing to be professional.

But her song was not sweet and later when she said to the wounded soldier, "I could show you the park," feeling danger and pleasure and fear all at once in her own words, he looked back at her coldly. Was it the words of the song? Or because she knew nothing of war while he, six years older, had been destroyed by it? Or because he preferred her friend?

"You were flirting with him, Amber," Myra said, sitting on the stairs with her, eating macaroons. Amber couldn't explain that she wanted to make him feel better. Nor did she tell how she had lain down beside him on the grass and how after a few moments he had pushed her from him and stood up and walked away. Walked down the aisle with Myra. Stayed around Myra's house for years to recover from his wounds.

Around her they were twittering like birds: *Marlene Dietrich is dead*. Repeating it over and over in chorus. Amber cupped her hands over her ears like seashells and heard her father crying.

All the foreigners were leaving. The trains were full of French families and Italians and Belgians making for the coast. The Germans had gone months before. Mother stayed in the drawing room beside the hated sewing box. Outside, on the top step, Father stood watching. In the hard soil, bleeding heart and daisies grew without care. The Swiss woman's sharp features softened to sorrow, perhaps guilt. In her smart brown coat and matching hat she was going home to her neutral mountains. Amber standing behind her father, wondered whether to pick a bouquet of the red and white flowers from the bed by the wall and offer them to the departing guest.

But then he cried out, like a seagull, "Aren't any of you going to say you're sorry she's going?"

It was too late. Her taxi door had closed and Miss

Rösle was no more than a hand waving, disappearing down the road. Father was wearing a smart blue chalk-stripe suit with a perfect crease and a starched collar and a tie. Dapper was the word. He was dapper and the foreign woman was leaving and his heart was cracking. Amber had almost heard it. Mother was nowhere to be seen. Had found something else to do. Loudly on the radio, a band was playing, "Here's to the next time." And the fighting had begun soon after. As if, by going back, the Swiss woman had started the war.

Marlene Dietrich is dead. They told her Marlene Dietrich had died and right away she heard her sister Jessie singing. They were standing side by side and Mother was hissing at them, *Turn out your toes, stand straight.* They were wearing dresses made of blue taffeta, dresses with wide sashes and bows down the front. She began to sing but couldn't hear Jess. She made it through the first verse alone, *I am the naughty Lola.*

Instead of the usual applause a single voice cried out, "Shut up!"

Amber and her friend Myra will now render (short laugh from father), "You are my Sunshine." They stood hand in hand and sang together till her own voice cracked like a boy's and she put on her Dad's hat and learned about sex.

Myra had a sweeter voice but couldn't carry a tune in a bucket.

The boat called *Mercedes* carried them upstream. It was a day for ice cream. London was hot. And later they stood outside the theatre, waiting. Loitering was what her mother might have called it. She was standing outside a theatre wishing her name was up in lights, waiting to see if the lights would change formation and

spell out her name a foot high. Jess said it was her fault
for marrying a Greek. They would never put her name
up because they couldn't spell it. The lamp was shining down cone-shaped, lighting up the space beneath.

"She'll come out that way."

The crowd stood there, watching, waiting.

A big black car drew up and she said, "You'll see.
You'll see. Now you'll see her."

The star swept out, glittering sparks of light dancing off her silver lamé dress, her hair like gold thread.
She was princess of the world. Her smile was an embrace, and Amber knew that if she had run forward, the
star would have held her and kept her forever.

"She's not a good woman," Jess said.

But what did 'good' mean if it wasn't that promise
of love she'd seen in the star's eyes? *I am here*, she
seemed to say, *and you are mine.*

"She dreams she's back in England. Did she ever get
back?"

Amber didn't hear the answer. She didn't care. She
knew exactly where she was and it was none of their
business.

She followed the man who pretended to eat carpets.
Wilson and Keppel and the new Betty waited in the
wings ready to push their sandbox onto the stage as
soon as she came off. The Alhambra! The name held a
promise of oriental magic but for all the red plush out
in front, the place smelled of dust and wood shavings
backstage. She shared her dressing room with three
tap-dancers from Leeds who wore a perfume called
"Evening in Paris." The man in the black suit who had
just tried to kiss her pushed her forward with a don't-
let-us-down, and there she was, centre stage, nodding

to another man in a black suit just as she had once nodded to her mother.

Right after the war, the people needed entertainment. She was billed as *Our Own Marlene*. "Our own Marlene" was led onstage by the man in the black suit who had just tried to kiss her in the wings. She put on her trilby, brushed her hands down the sides of her trousers, patted her white shirt and was ready. She moved into the spot, leaned up against the fake lamp post, not too hard in case it fell over and made the audience laugh, and began to sing: "Underneath the lamplight, by the barrack square."

They sat there rapt. Servicemen and women, wives and children. People moved to tears by a simple song.

The war was over but the Swiss woman never came back. Philip made a brief appearance. Or was it Peter? Peter whom she loved who married Myra who never forgave her. Philip standing in the kitchen, a kitchen detached from a house, chopping parsley for tabouleh, turning on her, shouting, "I am not Greek enough for that," when she brought Steven home to stay.

The final tour of *Keep the Home Fires*. Last performance. An old town dating back a thousand years. She was singing in a hall that had once been a home to "naked and starving beggars." There was applause, tears, and a ticket to another country. A single one-way ticket to a place called Canada.

Philip went to Greece on his own. Greece? Timbuktu? At any rate he had gone and not returned and she had no idea where he was. She sat in the old timbered square, the wooden buildings built in the time of Shakespeare, and considered the future.

"This country is big," they said by way of welcome when the boat docked at a city on a river. "You'll soon find your way about." And she answered, "I have friends here."

"Come in. Come in." Myra was delighted to see her at first. But soon saw in her not one person but two. At the end of a week's visit as Peter stared at her, prompted her to sing, and offered to take her out in a canoe on the nearby lake, Amber felt Myra grow distant. Peter could recite lines of poetry. As the paddle touched the water, he murmured, "'Give me of your bark oh birch tree,'" and Amber had cried in his arms and left without giving Myra an address. She had left because Peter couldn't remember the rest of the poem.

Myra, singing out of tune as usual, had found her, was standing there now with a young woman she said was her daughter. Hers and Peter's. *Child of moonlight. Child of starlight.*

They told her Marlene Dietrich was dead and she heard applause. From the South and the North. West and East. The sound, like a strong sea, was about to sweep her off her feet and engulf her, close over her head. *They love you. They love you.* She bowed and smiled at an audience in a theatre so small it seemed no bigger than a Punch-and-Judy box. And in another so large it held millions. The faces all turned towards her. One she picked out. Peter? Philip? and went towards him till someone took her arm and led her back to her place.

"She wanders!" she heard someone at stage left say. "She's wandering again."

Amber smiled, pleased that they could have no idea where she was at any given moment. She smiled and nodded. She ignored them and got back on the train from Leeds to Skipton. Very soon the stark remains of the abbey would appear behind the trees. She sank back into the comfortable padded seat.

They had lied to her again. Marlene Dietrich was not dead. Her voice, with an orchestra behind it, was coming nearer and nearer. Her dress reflected coloured light from a chandelier.

"She's singing," the chirping voices said.

And the words of the song became clear, entirely filling the space, as the man in the dark suit who had just tried to kiss her led Amber Papadakis onto the stage of the Alhambra for her final encore.

PLAYING SCRABBLE WITH VLADIMIR NABOKOV

I ended his *dream* with a *t*, and added *ca*, spelling *cat*, scoring fourteen, widening the gap between us.

Vlodya was in his plump phase. He'd given up smoking and was sucking candy all the time and slipping the wrappers into his pocket so that he could look at them later in case coded messages were written on the inside. He was on the wrong train. So was I but didn't know it at the time.

He added *h,e,t,u,s* to my *cat* reaching the red square at the edge of the board and scored forty-two.

"What kind of word is that?" I asked, thinking to have caught him out at last.

He was watching a moth that had settled into the fold of the window blind and was probably also on the wrong train.

"It's a line," he said. "A straight line falling on to another straight line. It can also be spelt with a *k*."

I set down an *l* on one side of the *a* in *dream* and added *n,c,e* on the right of it, scoring five and beginning to nourish hope.

He was groping in his inside pocket for the fiftieth time. In New York the day before, marvelling at the tall buildings, he had stumbled on felons who had relieved him of his travelling plans, his cash, and the lecture he was to deliver in a town he was getting farther away from by the minute.

We had first met on a day long ago in Berlin when I was still a girl, nothing remarkable, and Lola-Lola was not even conceived. We were sitting side by side in the director's anteroom. Vlodya had been showing me patterns in the tiled floor with his foot. We had no common language then.

He laughed suddenly aloud and added *r,e,z,e,m,b* to my *lance* at a score of twenty-five.

"It's spelled with an *s*," I said. "I'm sure of it."

"Certainly not," he replied, apprehending the moth and putting it carefully into his handkerchief. "In any case, the *s* and the *z* are often interchangeable."

"Not in this case," I cried out. "Think of *resemble*, think of *semblance*.'

"*Zemblance*," he replied looking as though his thoughts were in the far-off land he had once called home.

And to which he had promised to take me one winter. Wrapped in soft fur, we would speak of eternity while the sledge glided softly over melting snow.

I shuffled my letters on the little stand. The train gathering speed, shook.

Vlodya and I had met again in Paris, in 1939, both of us packing to leave. And now, by chance, nineteen years later we were on a train out of Grand Central Station. It seemed like destiny.

Triumphantly I added *love* to the *c* of *cathetus*.

The train might take us to a new life, leaving behind old ties and bonds. Memory would speak for me. In the evening, I would sing for him.

Vlodya looked at my *love* for several minutes and after a time added *e,r,a*, below the *v* accumulating twenty-one points.

"It's a proper name," I complained.

"It's truth," he answered.

I set down my *s* and *d* either side of his *a* and lost count of the score.

When the train pulled into the next unwanted station, he got out with his bag and the moth and my desire.

I stayed on board with my case full of music and made words out of letters till the scenery took my breath away and it was really night.